W9-CHL-907

Diary

of an

emotional

idiot

Diary

of an

emotional

idiot

a novel

Maggie Estep

Harmony Books/New York

Published by Harmony Books, a division of Crown Publishers, Inc., 201 East 50th Street, New York, New York 10022. Member of the Crown Publishing Group.

Random House, Inc. New York, Toronto, London, Sydney, Auckland

http://www.randomhouse.com/

Harmony and colophon are trademarks of Crown Publishers, Inc.

Printed in the United States of America

Design by Lynne Amft

Library of Congress Cataloging-in-Publication Data

Estep, Maggie.
Diary of an emotional idiot: a novel/by Maggie Estep.—1st ed.
   I. Title.
PS3555.S754D53 1997   96-29203
813′.54—dc20   CIP

ISBN 0-517-70179-0

10 9 8 7 6 5 4 3 2 1

First Edition

For
Gene Estep

acknowledgments

Shaye Areheart for invaluable faith and help.

Jenny Meyer and her cohort Stewart Meyer for feeding me and egging me on.

M. Doughty—you were right.

Christopher Wool for that special piece of furniture.

Shahram Victory, Rick Moody, Carla Friedman, Matt Cook, Sean McNally, and John S. Hall for inspiring correspondence.

Troy Fuss, "The Boxer" and editorial adviser.

Mike Tyler for trying to help excise "As If."

Bliss Biggs. (Where are you? Please write or call at once.)

Nancy Murray for life itself and the O.E.D.,
Neil Christner;
Beautiful Ellen Murray and her ill-fitting pants, too;
My first audience: Jon Murray and Chris Murray.

Susan Edwards, the late David Rattray, Andrei Cordrescu, and especially Bob Holman for their early faith.

Sally King for that one driving lesson and for friendship.
Julia Murphy for beautiful friendship.
Mark Ashwill for fondling in movie theaters.
Marc Maron and Michael Portnoy for comic relief.

SOMEWHERE IN MY ABDOMEN
WAS A SAC OF WARM CARING,
A BLADDER OF EMOTIONAL NUTRITION,
DISTENDED WITH THE URGE
TO BURST AND ENGENDER
ANOTHER'S HEART.

—Will Self

prologue

Hello, my name is Zoe and this is my book. It is a document of Emotional Idiocy told in two parts. There is the "then" part,—which explains how I got here, and there is the "now" part, which documents what I am doing here. Although, of course, I don't know exactly what I'm doing here. At the moment, I am sitting at my desk naked but for some men's boxer shorts and many silver bracelets. I like to see myself in men's underwear. I like to see men in men's underwear. Men in women's underwear is also acceptable. Other women in men's underwear doesn't do so much for me. However, if someone were to bring a tribe of women clad only in men's underwear to my house, I might find it slightly exciting. I might not kick them out of my house.

My house is not a house. It is a small hovel in a tenement building on East Sixth Street in New York City. I live there with few furnishings, many books, and a cat named Wimpy given to me by Jim, a talented but ornery painter I used to sleep with. Wimpy weighs twenty-two pounds and has a psychological disorder: If I leave him alone too long, he becomes convinced that he has fleas and scratches himself raw. This I am telling you because it is an apt metaphor for how I feel in my skin right now. I am digging at my hide, rubbing it raw because I've been rubbed raw by love gone wrong. Yes. This is another tale of love gone wrong. This is me turned idiot in the face of human interaction.

1

Lungs and Company

Directly downstairs from me lives Lonette, a woman with the lung power of Pavarotti. Every day, I hear her shouting at her kids, "You stupid idiots, get in the motherfucking house and shut up." The kids in turn call each other motherfucker in higher octaves. The seven-year-old calls the two-year-old motherfucker and the two-year-old runs down the hallway naked, smeared in dirt and yelling, "Motherfucker, motherfucker, motherfucker," in his soprano squeak.

A while back, after Jim the Painter but before the two loves that have brought me to you bleating and yelping, I had a boyfriend named Edgar. Edgar always said white people didn't say motherfucker right. White people, Edgar said, said "Motherrfuck-er" in a way that conveyed nothing but pure whiteness. He tried to teach me to say it right. I don't. I can't. I'm white.

Lonette, the lady downstairs, says it right and says it loud. So do her kids. Theirs is not a subtle familial love. But it is love.

When the mailman comes, Lonette sashays into the hall to watch him distribute the mail. She wears a large T-shirt that partially covers the way her fake designer jeans define each cheek of her ass. I hear her fifty-cent flip-flops whip the hallway floor as she goes to glare at the mailman. She doesn't trust him. I don't either. In fact, I like to think of the mailman as a vicious cyborg. He will kill us all if we're not careful.

The mailman has tiny rust-colored eyes and a doughy undefined face flecked with large freckles. He has a robotic way of flipping letters into each of the twenty-four slots for the twenty-four apartments in our building. He does not respond to my saying hello. He does not respond to anyone saying hello. When Lonette's kids say, "Hi, motherfuckin' mailman," he just looks right through them.

When I haven't had enough sleep, which is most of the time, I start to see the mailman as a product of the kind of government experiment we like to pretend doesn't exist. The mailman is a cantankerous cyborg and my taxes are paying for him.

Lonette doesn't pay taxes. She's on welfare and she gives blow jobs for ten dollars. This I know because she has sung it in a fevered contralto to her two-year-old son, Ralphie: "Motherfucker, I'm out there sucking dick for ten dollars and you gotta go and make noise when I come home? What the fuck is wrong with you, Ralphie? Shut up and get in the house."

Once in a while, Lonette gets a letter from a guy who lives in Montreal and this, I discovered, is what keeps her going. She cornered me by the mailbox one day. "Girl," she said, "did you get any of my mail in your box? I'm looking for my letter. I know that motherfuckin' mailman put it in the wrong box. Girl, look and see if you didn't get it." I hadn't. In my box were just the usual bills and threats. There are plenty of these right now. My current job is as a part-time receptionist at a dungeon. I take orders from a formidable dominatrix named Belle. I am not sufficiently versed in sadism to become an actual dominatrix but have enough of a fondness for it to answer a dungeon's phones.

The guy in Montreal is the father of at least one of Lonette's kids. I heard her telling this to Daisy, the stripper who lives upstairs. Lonette and Daisy frequently have voluble heart-to-hearts while standing in the stairwell a few feet away from my own door. Daisy and Lonette are my personal soap opera.

One day, Daisy told Lonette she was thinking about leaving New York. "I'm gettin' sick of this shithole, you know? I pay a fucking thousand dollars to live in cockroach soup, you know?"

"You pay a thousand dollars?" Lonette said.

"Yeah, a fucking thousand dollars, and the other night I'm making tomato soup and I go to stir it and there's fucking not one but THREE roaches in my soup."

"Girl, you're stupid, you paying too much rent. Last person lived in your apartment paid like seventy-five dollars or something. Old white guy. Had him a rabbit. Guy was a mothahfucken freak. But he didn't pay no thousand dollars."

"Yeah, well, what am I gonna do? You wanna tell me that? I mean this shit's better than *Florida*, you know?"

"I ain't been to Florida, but shit, they got sunshine there, right?"

"Yeah, sunshine. That doesn't do me any good. Gimme skin cancer. Make my fucking face fall off. Florida sucked. The only place to dance was this bar called Rudy's Booty. Nobody with teeth went in that place. I'd be dancing my fucking FACE off for these ninety-year-old guys that just grinned gums at me. No fun, right? Then I come up here but it's unreal, there's all these nineteen-year-olds with tits that stand up and say hello, and like I can't compete with that, so then I end up dancing out in fucking QUEENS and shit, like I get stuck with the day shift in QUEENS. I mean, what kind of shit is that?"

"Yeah, I hear you," Lonette said then, "but that ain't as bad as me. I'm in love with a guy that's got no ass and he lives in Montreal He's my son Ralphie's daddy," she said.

This was as much of the exchange as I heard because then Lonette invited Daisy to come in and smoke a joint. I heard the metronomic clicking of Daisy's fuck-me pumps as she teetered into Lonette's hovel.

I am not, as I may have conveyed, a complete eavesdropping loner. I do have friends. I do have a lover: The Reader. This moniker because, the second time we slept together, right after we had had rigorous and delicious sex, I grabbed a book I was reading, showed it to The Reader, and asked, "Have you read this?" At which he flapped his beautiful blue eyes and said, "How would you feel if I told you I never

5

read?" Not terribly surprised, I thought. But what I said was, "Oh, that's okay. I guess a lot of people don't read." When I relayed this to my closest friend, Jane, she said, "Ah, well, now we know what to call him. He is The Reader."

The Reader is physically beautiful but emotionally stunted, which is about all I can handle at this juncture. He is twenty-five and he is from a small town in Washington. His mother works in a candy store and, once a month, sends The Reader packages of candy. The Reader is a drummer. I am a bass player. I am a terrible bass player. In spite of this, I was briefly in a band that made money. It was a fluke, though. The Reader is a good drummer. All the same, he earns most of his living working as a busboy. The Reader is my lover. He is not really a friend. I have friends for that.

This might be a good moment to confess that I have literary ambitions. I write fuck books. Sort of high-minded porn. Occasionally, I even write poetry. About my neighbors. "The Decline of Eye Guy" is one I am currently at working on. Eye Guy is the speed freak in the apartment directly next door to me. He lives with his girlfriend. Although her eyes don't bulge the way Eye Guy's do, for facility's sake, I call her Eye Girl. Eye Girl is very moody. She is always zooted up on some really foul combination of uppers and downers and Rollerblading. Her bouts of Rollerblading seem to coincide with fights with Eye Guy. I hear them scream at each other, and next thing, Eye Girl is on Rollerblades and making her way down the stairs. Eye Girl is friends with Lonette and Daisy. On good days, she sticks her head out the door of her and Eye Guy's apartment and screams: "LONETTE, GET YOUR UGLY ASS UP HERE AND GIVE ME FIVE DOLLARS, MY CHECK FROM MY MOTHER DIDN'T COME."

On bad days, she walks downstairs, bangs on Lonette's door, and says, "You fucking junkie cunt, open the fucking door right now."

I am not sure why Lonette, a welfare mother, gives Eye Girl, a trashy twentyish white girl, money. I don't think I want to understand that particular economy.

One day, the Cyborg Mailman did in fact put Lonette's letter from Montreal into the wrong box. The Cyborg Mailman put the letter from Montreal into the Heavy Metal Guitarist Upstairs's box.

I heard the very polite Japanese fashion students from upstairs standing in the stairwell telling it to Daisy the Stripper.

"Yes," the Japanese students were saying, "the man who play White Zombie over and over, that man he was very drunk and he defecate in hallway."

"Oh God, that's REALLY gross," Daisy said.

"Yes, and then he set fire to couch and firemen come and lady from downstairs came up to see what commotion was and see a letter for her is in apartment of Heavy Metal Guitarist and there is shit on letter."

"Oh my God. He SHIT on one of her precious letters from Montreal?" Daisy's voice rose an octave.

"Yes," the students said in unison. They are a boy and a girl and they often talk at the same time, as if they were the same person. As if they were Japanese Siamese Twin Fashion Students.

At this point I went out into the hall, said hello to Daisy, and nodded at the Japanese Siamese Twins. They nodded back in unison.

"You heard about how Mikey shit in the hall and set his couch on fire?" Daisy asked me then.

"Yeah, well, I just overheard you talking about it. That guy's nuts, man."

The Japanese Siamese Twins giggled.

"Oh, Mikey's not nuts, he's just drunk. I used to date him," Daisy said then.

"You did?" The twins and I in unison.

"Yeah, for two weeks. We were like sort of in love, but then he went on a bender and got like this HEAD WOUND from passing out at the Bronx Zoo because he gets drunk and he likes to go look at pandas and then he got too drunk and fell over and like crashed into some lady's wheelchair and hurt his head and then he broke up with me."

She said it like it happens every day. Every day a guy drunkenly swoons for pandas and every day a guy gets a head wound and breaks up with a stripper who danced for toothless men in the Everglades.

Just as Daisy was nonchalantly relaying this detail of her lurid love life, Lonette emerged from her apartment. She was dragging two-year-old Ralphie by the arm. "Motherfucker, you're coming to the store with me," she was saying. Then she noticed all of us standing there and, at that very moment, the Cyborg Mailman came in and all hell broke loose.

The Cyborg Mailman saw us all standing there, but still he ignored us.

Lonette drew herself up to her full height and said, "MOTHER-FUCKER, YOU PUT MY MOTHERFUCKIN' LETTER IN FUCKIN' DRUNK MIKEY'S BOX AND HE FUCKIN' SHIT ON MY LETTER."

The mailman didn't say anything. He began to open up the mailboxes but he was shaken. You could see it. His eyes darted nervously.

"MOTHERFUCKER," Lonette wailed, "I'M TALKING TO YOU. LOOK AT ME WHEN I'M TALKING TO YOU."

"Please don't raise your voice at me," the mailman said then.

"DON'T RAISE MY VOICE? WHAT ABOUT DON'T PUT MY LETTER IN THE WRONG BOX, WHAT ABOUT THAT?"

"Listen, lady, I'm sorry, I'm only human."

"No you're not," Lonette said then, "you're like a fuckin' robot, and shit, you're like the terminator of mailmen. Used to be we had us a nice mailman, now we got you, fuckin' T2, man."

I couldn't believe it. Lonette also thought the mailman was a cyborg. I was not alone. She, too, wanted to shake that mailman, drive some heart into his circuitry, make him see how putting the letter from Montreal into Mikey the Heavy Metal Guitarist's box had almost ruined everything, how that letter was what the Lady Downstairs needed, that letter made it all worthwhile, a multitude of dicks to suck and a bunch of kids to yell "motherfucker" at.

And then the Cyborg Mailman melted. First, his hands began to shake uncontrollably, then he actually DROPPED a huge stack of mail. It went fanning out all over the floor as all of us stood dumbfoundedly witnessing the cracking of the cyborg facade. And then he started to cry. His puffy white features mushed together like malevolent cookie dough and tears came out of his rust-colored eyes.

Then he doubled over and wailed out, "I'M SORRY I'M SORRY I'M SORRY."

We were all shocked. Not one of us said a word. It was so uncharacteristic that we didn't have a clue as to what our lines should be.

And then the mailman just turned around and walked back down the greasy hall and out the door. He just left. He left the mailbag and everything. The mailman just walked out of the building.

We never found out what was wrong with him. We talked about it. Everyone did. Daisy and Lonette and the Japanese Siamese Twins and even Mikey the fecally fixated Heavy Metal Guitarist. We all wondered what went wrong. You always hear about mailmen going nuts. Postal psychopaths are perfectly commonplace. But now it had happened to us.

We never saw the Cyborg Mailman again. We have a new mailperson. A woman named Lucy. She is short, Puerto Rican, and loves to talk. She and Lonette talk about the Guy From Canada and how he has no ass. One day the Heavy Metal Guitarist asked Lucy what had happened to the old mailman but Lucy didn't know.

Last week, I came in and saw that Daisy had cornered Lucy the Mailwoman and was pouring her heart out to her: "Yeah, so then I was naked in front of these toothless guys in the Everglades, and they were like grinning GUMS at me and like . . ." she trailed on as Lucy the Mailwoman nodded sympathetically and continued to stick the mail in the slots. Maybe I should confide my heartaches to Lucy the Mailwoman. But I'm not like that. I'd rather tell them to you.

9

2

Feed Me

Charlie, my father, was a vagabond horse trainer. As a kid, he hopped freights and hitchiked across the U.S. He took up with a rodeo, worked as a mechanic, then was drafted into Korea where he jumped out of airplanes. One day, on a routine mission, a sergeant miscalculated. My father was told to jump at the wrong time. He landed in a truck bed in a parking lot and fractured most of his body. He spent several months hospitalized in Korea. He lay prone in a full body cast, being fed nutrients and morphine through an IV. After a few months, he was discharged, and, still in the cast, put on a plane home. They neglected to detox him and a few hours into the journey the opiates started spitting out of his system in whirling spasms of pain. By the time the plane landed stateside, my father felt more physical pain than he thought a human body would endure.

He never forgave the ubiquitous "Them" for this neglect and, from that moment on, veered as far away from governing bodies as possible. This somehow led him to horse training. He had been working as a mechanic and was called to fix farm trucks on a rich guy's estate. The guy's daughter, a whispy sixteen-year-old with an upturned nose, was riding a horse near the garage. The girl was having trouble. Charlie, who'd mastered breaking horses in his rodeo days, saw the girl struggling and volunteered his help. This led to a job training the rich guy's horses. Which eventually led to Charlie's meeting Francine, my mother.

Francine had just finished high school where she'd graduated valedictorian. She was good-looking and composed. And she was a budding martyred saint of the work ethic. She shoveled shit at the rich guy's barn in exchange for riding some of his horses. Charlie chased Francine, and, although Charlie was wild and funny-looking, my composed mother fell for him hard. They were married and I arrived eight months later. Now Francine worked double time, taking care of me and helping Charlie shovel horse shit, train horses, and maintain the stable.

Working for rich people was hard on Charlie. Although he opposed institutions and most forms of government, he did have a had a sort of socialist streak: Wealth rubbed him the wrong way. He'd tolerate his various employers as long as he could and then one day we'd move. This caused a strain between Charlie and Francine and I could feel their relationship decaying fragmenting with each passing month. By the time I was four, they barely spoke to one another and I started running away from home. I wasn't very good at it and never got far but the urge to run was strong.

We moved from New Jersey to Pennsylvania to Canada, then, when I was six, to Upstate New York. We lived in a little apartment above the stables. I was in first grade but hung around with a girl named Mimi who was eleven and lived in a sprawling house across the street. I don't remember all that much about Mimi except that she had curly hair and I wanted her life. I also appreciated the fact that she and her family seemed to tolerate me and let me spend a lot of time in their house, eating their food and watching their big TV.

By this time, Francine and Charlie were sort of distant figures in my life. They were always working while I wandered around outside or imposed myself on strangers. At school, I'd taken to beating up boys I had crushes on. And stealing girls' lunch money. This I did just for the thrill. I didn't have any use for their nickels. But I took them.

One day, Francine said we were moving and Charlie wasn't coming with us. I was surprised but went along with it. We moved into her friend Harriet's apartment. Harriet was a dog breeder and was away on the dog show circuit. Her apartment was a hideous kitsch dog inferno: doggy-patterned rugs, bath towels, and plates and, everywhere, large posters, engravings, and paintings of poodles, who were apparently Harriet's breed of choice. I was sitting in the living room one day, under a gilt-framed poodle painting, when Francine told me she was going to Mexico to get a divorce from Charlie. I shrugged at this news, not exactly sure what it would mean. Would we continue to live in Doggy Inferno? And if not, where would we go? What would Charlie do? Did he care?

These questions were answered two weeks later when Francine told me to pack, we were moving. We went to her new boyfriend's house. His name was Henry. He was tall, bald, and spoke in a deep, flat monotone. He was a microbiologist and certainly looked the part. Small glasses, a thick ginger beard, and eyes that appeared to have difficulty focusing upon the banality of mortals.

Francine and I settled into Henry's house, which was a quaint mock log cabin affair. I slept in the living room and, at Henry's insistence, began wearing my previously moppish hair in two tidy pigtails.

I saw my father infrequently. When Francine did drop me off to spend a day with him, he would pick me up in his arms, loosen my pigtails, then take me to feed on ice cream, candy, and other snacks. By the time Francine fetched me at the end of the day, I had dreadlocks and was covered in multicolored food stains .

One day, Francine and Henry sat me down and said: "Zoe, we are moving to France."

"We are? Why?"

"I've been offered a job there," Henry said. "France is in Europe, it is very cultured. You will like it there."

"Ah," I said. A few days later, Henry and Francine dropped me off at Charlie's house. I was to say my good-byes. I was going to France. I did not like the idea of France. But I thought Francine would be upset if I tried to stay with Charlie, so I said good-bye to Charlie, who showered me with bracelets and horse pictures and held me tight for one uncharacteristic moment. A few days later, I left for France with Francine and Henry.

We moved to Versailles, a suburb of Paris and, of course, home to Louis XIV's ostentatious palace. We had a big white house with a rose garden. It was almost as big as my friend Mimi's house had been. I should have been happy but there were some problems. One was that Francine and Henry decided it was best that I go to a French school. They figured I'd just learn French by osmosis.

I did learn the language quickly but didn't let on to my teachers because the things they wanted us to do were tedious. I feigned complete idiocy in class and chased boys during recess. I had one girlfriend, Frederique, who was at my side at all times. As I chased and beat the boys up, Frederique stood by watching and smirking and grinning her approval. Frederique had lovely parents who let me spend a fair amount of time visiting their apartment. There, I was in heaven. We could watch TV and listen to the radio, things Henry and Francine forbade.

Soon Henry's Regime of Terror began. I was browbeaten for bad grades, humiliated for poor posture, and endlessly chided for what they called my surly disposition. I was not only assigned an endless array of horrible household chores—straightening the fringe on the rugs, polishing the dinner table, dusting the attic—but was forbidden to leave the house other than to go to school. For recreation, Henry one day installed a bookshelf full of voluminous tomes, in French. Proust, Molière, even Rimbaud, but only Camus stole my heart. I fell in love with *L'Étranger* and made it through most of *La Peste.* This served to make me even surlier. I stared for hours at Camus's author photos and cultivated a brooding look.

My brooding, accompanied by an exaggerated slouching walk, caused Henry to one day hand me a tutu and tell me I was going to ballet school. His withering eyes sparkled as he hurled the word *ballet* at me.

And so, the next day, I skulked off to ballet school. I arrived a few minutes late and snarling. The teacher told me to find a space for myself at the barre. I then stood, one hand on the barre, a besotted ballerina before me, another behind me, and plié'ed. After a half hour of this buffoonery, I actually found myself enjoying it. A Chopin adagio was playing, and I had broken a sweat and felt slightly adrenalized.

Soon, to Henry and Francine's surprise, I was the star ballet pupil. I twirled and twonked and pirouetted my face off. Eventually, I talked Frederique into joining up. We went to ballet each day after school, then, as soon as we were done, skulked around and smoked cigarettes.

When I was eleven, Francine got pregnant and, for some reason, we moved from the big house to a small apartment. This didn't make any sense that I could figure, especially when my twin half brothers, Julian and James, were born. I liked Julian and James immensely. For one thing, they diverted Henry and Francine's attention from whatever ostensibly bad stuff I was up to, and for another thing, Julian and James were cute and very well-mannered babies. And, thanks to their many infant needs, I was soon able to be out of the house for long stretches of time without Henry noticing.

Our apartment was right near the grounds of the Château of Versailles, and so, when I wasn't at ballet class, I was wandering around the endless gardens. My friend, Frederique, sometimes accompanied me, but mostly I wandered on my own, the better to take in the blossomings and whisperings of the ornately landscaped place.

I continued on at Catholic school, beating up boys I liked and getting in trouble with the nuns. One day, when a boy named Jean Baptiste and I were caught in a bathroom feeling each other's hairless genitals, I got sent to the head nun's office. Her name was Soeur De France. She was a thin, bony thing with orange skin and hair. "Zoheee," she said raspingly, "tu es *salle*" She spat out the word *salle*, and her shit-smelling breath wafted around me, making me think of the putrescent stink of Jesus' decomposed corpse.

After forcing me to admit that I was indeed a filthy little troll,

Soeur De France smiled and seemed to be on the verge of dismissing me. Then she said, "Zoh-eee, don't you find my name, De France, to be beautiful?"

I couldn't believe it. A *nun* blowing her own horn. What about effacement of self, what about *humility*? I said that no, De France was really not a remarkable name. This was the straw that busted old De France's back. She put me in the retard class then. It was me, the little American freak, and some mongoloids and paraplegics and a Portuguese girl with elephantiasis. We were not so much learning-disabled as just plain odd in the eyes of the head num.

We sat around doing Catholic Art Therapy. One day, the town's TV news team came to do a special on us retards and how, for all our learning disabilities, we were making progress and would become upstanding French citizens after all. As a demonstration of our accomplishments, they shot several seconds of *me*, painting. I was making an abstract portrait of two nuns having lesbian sex—something Frederique and I had halfheartedly forayed into. The painting looked rather pretty with swirls of pink and black that the TV crew interpreted as floral, not sexual. When I went home, I snuck into the living room where the TV sat, mostly unused. I was not allowed to watch it and so had to covertly catch the news program. And, sure enough, there it was, me and my painting of dyke nuns, on national French TV. Maybe this was where I got the notion to indirectly make money off of sex. I had painted nuns going at it and there I was on TV. It was a slow but natural evolution to my present-day occupation as fuck book writer and receptionist to dominatrixes.

3

Idiots Anonymous

Yesterday we had another of our Idiots Anonymous dinners.

Idiots Anonymous is what me and a few of my friends call ourselves. It started with Oliver the Bassoon Player and Merle the Poet. Oliver used to be a crack addict. Merle and I were both dope fiends. One night, we got into swapping stories over dinner. Sort of the way they do in AA or NA or Whatever A. Only with us it's completely informal and extremely cynical. We started doing it about a year ago. Sometimes other friends would come. They all had to have been dope fiends or sex addicts or thieves or something. And they had to tell us their funny or apalling stories.

One day, Oliver, having relayed a particularly desperate story, said, "We really are idiots, aren't we?"

To which Merle said, "Yeah, we're big anonymous idiots swimming through a baffling world. We should just call ourselves Idiots Anonymous." And so we did.

A few nights ago, Oliver called and told me there was going to be an Idiots Anonymous dinner. I said I didn't think I could make it. I just didn't feel like it. The Reader was coming over.

The Reader came carrying a pint of ice cream. The Reader loves to eat ice cream. "So, how are you?" I asked as he flipped the lid off the Häagen-Dazs and started jabbing the frozen pint with a spoon.

"Oh, I'm all right. I'm tired. I dunno." He kissed me, putting an end to the small talk. We rolled around on the couch. I pulled at his tongue stud with my teeth.

Although I can appreciate the concept of piercing and poking holes all over yourself just as well as I can appreciate the feeling of superiority my friend Fanny, a member of Idiots Anonymous, feels when she mutilates herself, taking a razor blade to her chest and stomach, then walking around with oozing wounds under her clothing, this secret somehow giving her an edge, a one-up on everyone else, although I can appreciate all this in theory, I don't do it to myself. But I do enjoy biting The Reader's tongue stud, pulling on it, watching him wince as the mixture of pain and pleasure spirals through his receptors.

The Reader couldn't stay long, though. He had to run off to work. He is a busboy. We satisfied ourselves with heavy petting and then The Reader rezipped his pants, tightened his tongue stud, and went to work.

When he left I started to feel gray. Gray being infinitely worse than black or white. It was still early. The Idiots were probably still at Passage to India, having dinner and swapping stories. I decided to go look for them.

They had already eaten. They greeted me and I sat down just as Merle launched into a food story. Merle's compulsions have scurried up the food chain of addiction so that he now devours enormous vats of Ben & Jerry's instead of pumping his scarred arms full of heroin.

"I got a call from an ex-girlfriend and it kind of made me feel fucked up and I ate . . . uh . . . I ate a *lot*," Merle said. "Actually, this is really embarrassing, but I live in Brooklyn, right, so I had to drive to get to the supermarket that has the kind of ice cream I like, right? So I drive over there. I buy THREE pints of Ben & Jerry's *and* a bag of cookies. I go back to my car and I can't wait till I get home, so I just start doggin' this stuff right there in the parking lot. Pretty soon I feel really, really sick. I'm just gonna blow up and spray all over the place, right? So then I started HATING myself. I got so mad I HURLED the ice cream out the window, put the car in drive, and RAN OVER THE ICE CREAM."

We all laughed with commiseration. I could picture Merle, in his ubiquitous stained sweatsuit, ice cream drooling down his chin and painting his chest. His pale eyes are at half mast, the sugar courses through him, sedating him, lulling him into a gentle fat world. Then, heroically, Merle shakes off the demons of mass consumption and sends the ice cream containers sailing out the window. Puts the car in drive. Backs up. Fertilizes the parking lot's cement with creamy goo.

I had been there. So had everyone else at the table. If not with three pints of Ben & Jerry's per se, then scalding ourselves on crack pipes, shivering through a neon dawn of promiscuity, or shuffling down greasy corridors of self-hatred, gambling, shopping, shooting, or simple ill-advised adoration of psychopaths and sluts. Yes, we had metaphorically been there with Merle and three pints of Ben & Jerry's sliming down his intestinal tract.

"So then," Merle continued, "I went back home, right? And I got pretty depressed. I was fat *and* I had guilt about this ex-girlfriend. She was really pretty good to me back then, you know? She was a really nice girl and I just lied to her all the time and even one time, one time she was trying to get me to kick heroin and I wouldn't, so she like *chained* me, I swear, she CHAINED me to the bed, and padlocked me and everything. Then she went to work, but as soon as she left, I noticed she had stupidly left the key to the padlock on a chair near the bed and I wiggled my foot around and knocked the key off the chair, then managed to bend down and get it and unlock the padlock. I went out and copped a bundle of dope. I came back and got totally fucked up and then wrapped the chain back around myself. She came home that night and couldn't figure out why I was so happy."

We all laughed hard.

"So, I don't know. It made me feel weird to hear from her. And now I feel fat and that makes me want to shoot dope, but I guess I won't." Merle looked at us all then. We were smiling. The waiter at that moment brought Oliver a dish of mango ice cream. Merle's eyes bulged. Oliver laughed.

"Okay, you guys, I got one," I said then. "I went to town on the self-loathing today."

"Yeah?" said Tina the Bulemic, her eyes lighting up with interest, for she is the queen of self-loathing.

"Yeah, I spent the whole day obsessing pointlessly. You know how you get when you can't stop obsessing over who your ex-boyfriend is fucking?"

Tina nodded gravely. Oliver smiled. Merle winced. David the Sex Addict grew more attentive. My friend Elizabeth, a drummer and former speed freak, looked at me knowingly. So did Jane, my closest friend, a former junkie and current porn writer. Elsie, a compulsive shoplifter, gnawed her fingernails.

"I saw someone who looked like my ex walking hand in hand with this girl with blue hair and a pierced face." I said then. Jane rolled her eyes. She had already heard about it. The others were attentive, though. "I mean, some people, fine—they're pierced, they're dyed, it's fine. They look good. But other people, they look like blue-haired idiots, you know? So this girl looked like a blue-haired idiot and she was walking with a guy that looked like my ex-boyfriend and then I became convinced my ex-boyfriend is fucking someone with blue hair. And this sent me over the edge. I even listened to Joy Division and turned off all the lights. It was ridiculous. I felt like an emotional sub-dwarf. So then I started obsessing over my *other* ex-boyfriend, the one I left the one who's fucking someone with blue hair for. He's a jerk. He dumped me cruelly. And I think of him fondly."

They all laughed hard at that one.

I went on, "I realize that this is all very pathetic and petty, but all the same, it got me in a FROTH. Then I went and bought a bunch of underwear for when my lover came over, but then he got there and I just sort of smelled emptiness, do you know what I mean?" I paused then. It seemed they did. They all knew the smell of emptiness.

"Then he left and I just felt myself falling, you know, just getting scooped out from the inside. Which makes me want to shoot dope."

Oliver put his arm around me and fed me a spoonful of ice cream.

David the Sex Addict started telling us how he had had his way with yet another unsuspecting Coke machine's change slot. He had, he told us, once read an article about a muscleman on steroids who got so horny he actually fucked the change slot in a Coke machine. This had stuck with David for a while and now he, too, was taking the pause that refreshes.

Tina the Bulemic had had a binge, which she described in exacting detail: three orders of mashed potatoes at the trendy eatery Lucky Strike, escargots, soufflé, and lamb paillard at Provence, more mashed potatoes, a burger, and Cajun fries at Acme, and half a pie of Death by Chocolate to Go from the Noho Star. Tina was, after all, no mere bulemic. No, she liked to binge at the trendiest of eateries, in the company of painters and art collectors, covertly making an utter pig of herself. She would schedule four or five different dinner dates, eating a fairly normal portion at each one. By the end of the night, she would stumble home, nearly catatonic until she purged into the porcelain.

Yes, we had all had our battles and now we spewed our brief narratives. At midnight the waiter brought our check. We paid up and then slowly made our way out onto the street.

Merle pulled his overcoat around his bulbous middle, then walked over to where he had parked his car, a beat-up Bug that belonged to his wife, a computer analyst and yoga practitioner who will only loan him the car if and when he goes down on her for approximately seventeen hours. David the Sex Addict and Elsie, the quiet compulsive shoplifter, skulked off together. Oliver and I fondled each other at the corner of Avenue B and Seventh Street. Oliver and I do this often. We used to be lovers and are still sexually attracted to and emotionally dependent on each other, but we refuse to love each other. We save that for people more different from us. People with whom we cannot possibly forge a lasting link. Still, we fondle, we hump, we kiss, we whistle through each other's voids.

"Baby," I said, resting my cheek on Oliver's shoulder.

"Aw," he said. Then: "I can't keep track, who are you still in love with, Satan or the other one?"

"Satan" was my tender moniker for the ex-boyfriend who dumped me. Satan, who, in order to get my attention, once ripped out the last pages of a series of detective novels I was reading. Satan, whose pointed features are in fact very devilish. Satan, flamboyantly tearing through my heart and leaving little cloven hoof marks upon it.

"Oh, I don't know," I told Oliver, "it's confusing. I loved Satan, but I loved Bev in a different way. But fuck them both, wanna come over?" This I asked knowing full well that Oliver, in a completely uncharacteristic move, has now vowed monogamy with Bonnie, a precocious twenty-one-year-old nymphomaniac quantum physicist.

"The only reason you want me is 'cause I'm trying to be monogamous," Oliver said then, squinching up his beautifully cragged face. He was, of course, right. We both knew this yet let our fingers linger on each other a few moments longer.

We applied lips, then went our separate ways.

In the hall of my building, two-year-old Ralphie was sitting on the stairs playing with a shard of broken glass. As I debated whether or not to actually intervene in Ralphie's potential disaster, the Lady Downstairs emerged from her hovel: "Motherfucker, where you at?" She saw her offspring, then: "Motherfucker, what the fuck you doin' with that? What are you, fuckin' stupid?" Ralphie smiled benignly and relinquished the shard. I walked up the stairs and into my own hovel.

I stood in the middle of the floor. Then I paced.

Maybe I would call Satan, Satan who lured me away from Bev, the ex-boyfriend who, I've now decided, is fucking a girl with blue hair. Satan, who, in spite of all this, I still want to call and see and touch; Satan, into whose depths I still want to dive, plundering glitzy trinkets and totems as if his soul were the crusty tomb of some minor Egyptian deity. Maybe I would call Satan while Oliver sat pathetically by his own phone, waiting for Bonnie the Brilliant Nympho to call from the pristine Massachusetts town where she is locked away, performing highly secret quantum physicist research. Bonnie, whose ability to come upward of thirty times in one day of epic fucking has now twisted the otherwise emotionally aloof Oliver into several knots of love.

Finally, I did it. I picked up the phone and dialed Satan's number. Satan was apparently out taking care of Important Satan Business. The answering machine clicked on. I hung up.

I started ogling my bicycle chain. I saw it in a new light. I saw it restraining poor Merle. Leaving sad red indentations in his fat. Of course, back then, back when Merle was being chained, he was probably not fat. The chain probably bruised his meatless junkie's ribs. I thought then of Satan's own meatless ribs. I thought of my bicycle chain bruising and restraining Satan as his nostrils flared out and spewed juice. I imagined yanking the chain tightly around him, digging into his flesh, leaving imprints on his corporeal self as he had left cruel metaphoric welts on the valves of my heart.

I picked my key ring up off my desk, walked over to where my bike was leaning against the closet door, unlocked the padlocks, and unfurled the great length of chain. I toyed with it for a minute. I had never thought of my bicycle chain this way. It was just an anti-theft device. Now I thought it would be perversely funny to at least think about taking it for a visit to Satan's house. I put the chain in a plastic garbage bag. I got the keys to Satan's house that I still had in my desk drawer. I went out to catch a cab over to his townhouse on West Eleventh Street.

The cabdriver's hack license told me his name was Muhammad Ali. This, then, would be the seventh Muhammad Ali cabdriver I had had in the past year. Muhammad Ali drove terribly. Pumping and choking the gas, running lights, hitting potholes, cursing in Arabic. Getting on the car radio and cursing in Arabic to his dispatcher, who then cursed back.

Muhammad Ali dropped me off in front of Satan's townhouse, then veered off into the night, raping another pothole as he went.

I rang the buzzer but there was no answer. I let myself in the vestibule, where all those awful German paintings hang. Paintings

Satan paid a pretty penny for, garrish blobs of olive green and orange splashed on enormous canvases. Satan's treasures. Satan is rich. He makes buckets of money off his own artwork, "sculptures" that are enormous shopping carts filled with discarded tools, signs, and dried foodstuffs smeared in paint. Satan got rich off shopping carts and now he lives the high life.

I went up to the second floor and stood looking at Satan's bed, a plain modern platform sheathed in austere white. I looked to see if there were any hideous stains anywhere, stains from fluids that had oozed out of some girl other than me. There were not. Of course, Satan is fastidious and it's unlikely that he would have left any stains there. He would have had his assistant, a mousy woman named Mary, carry the stained sheets off to a dry cleaner who would have gotten the goo out. I sniffed the sheets for evidence of dry cleaning or stain removal but found none. I stared at the bed. In this bed I had loved Satan. I had loved Satan in the bed and out of the bed. Mistake number one. I should have confined it to lust. Poor Bev was in Cincinnati, Ohio, the first night I went home with Satan. Bev was in a Days Inn in Cincinnati, Ohio, furiously E-mailing missives of love to me. And I was in bed with Satan. This much Bev and I could have survived. A quick bonk with the devil is one thing. Opening the treacherous valves of my heart to him was another. It was a mistake.

I went into Satan's large walk-in closet and sat there, on the nifty postmodern THING that is an excuse for furniture. I took the chain I had with me out of the big garbage bag I had it in and sat there with it on my lap and waited.

4

Kiss Me, I Ache

I was twelve when I first stuck my tongue in another human's mouth. His name was François and we had been at summer camp together. He was doughy and shy and, prior to the kiss, we'd had absolutely no interaction. He was a loner who chased and trapped bugs and butterflies. I sat next to him during the long bus ride home as all the other seats were taken. He sat clutching a briefcase, which, I soon discovered, housed his fastidious collection of bug carcasses. I looked across my nose as he softly fondled and arranged these corpses. They were stored in various glassine baggies and miniature jars that François had painstakingly labeled. François saw me eyeballing his specimens and, taking this as a come-on, asked if I like bugs. And suddenly, I did. I was enthralled with the dark brittle corpses and particularly with the pudgy hands that handled them. "Oh yes, yes," I said. There was an awkward pause then. Maybe he thought I was mocking him. I started asking questions about the bugs. "Hey, what does this one do?"

"Ah, interesting you should pick that one out. A rarity. A globiferous cockroach."

"Ah."

François was coming to life now, and in his excitement, he squeezed hard on the Globiferous Cockroach jar. Too hard. It shattered. Shards and bits scattered all over our seats and onto the floor.

We both got down on all fours, picking up the bits. François was shaken. Literally. His pudgy paw trembled. I assumed he was broken up over the roach. But then, he put his lips to mine. They were quivering lips. His mouth was warm and greasy and when his tongue came darting and seeking my own, I felt nausea and pleasure at once.

Eventually, François's paws wandered down into my T-shirt. His fingers tweeked my nipples, tweeked with extreme sensitivity, like they were bugs to be coaxed gently into a trap. And coax he did. It is miraculous that the camp counselors failed to notice any of this. Our breath, coming in hot twelve-year-old gasps, must have been steaming the interior of the entire bus. We rubbed against each other, we felt parts, we swapped fluids, we moaned and heaved and exhaled heated breaths like so many totems of nascent sexuality. Then, we were back in the city. As the bus pulled into the parking lot, I could see Francine standing in the parking lot, waiting for me. For a few more minutes I felt lecherous and alive then, François and I got off the bus, and, without looking each other in the eye, shook hands with the gravity of two people who have just had a passing exchange at a conference of oligists.

A few weeks later, before I'd had time to see my fair François again, Henry was assigned a job back in the States. We packed up our lives, I sadly bid farewell to Frederique, and we flew to Colorado.

We settled for three weeks in a Ramada Inn in Downtown Boulder, Colorado, while Henry and Francine looked for a place to live. They picked out a little log cabin on the side of a mountain an hour from town. The land was dry, the sky too big, and our cabin quite claustrophobic.

Soon, my half sister Louise was born and life in our strange little family revolved around Baby Louise's voluble infant needs. We were all scurrying around, even James and Julian. Louise was a screamer and a shitter and we were all endlessly cleaning, feeding, and amusing this little terror.

* * *

When Francine took me down to enroll in junior high school, the principal, finding my English rusty, put me in the special ed class. It was full of young burn-outs, among them Rina and Rosie Raggart, two redheaded twins who eventually took me under their wing.

One day, Rosie came up to me and said, "Zoe, the reason everybody hates you is 'cause you wear those flowered shirts all the time. You look weird."

"Oh," I said flatly. Rosie was no prize herself. Her face was covered in enormous brown freckles that mottled her skin, as if Jackson Pollock had had a go at her. I don't know where she got off mocking my finely tailored French shirts. But she did. She was brash and confident and thirteen.

"I like my shirts," I said finally. "They're from France."

"Is that what's wrong with you? You're from FRANCE?" Rosie said, scrunching up her face.

"France is beautiful," I said, defending the homeland. Rina and Rosie looked at each other and shrugged. After a few more similar exchanges, they took to me. Now I couldn't shake them if I wanted. And I didn't want. I was not, in general, winning popularity contests and I needed these two as friends.

Because I was surly, somber, and a C− student, Francine and Henry never let me accept the Raggarts' invitations to spend the weekend. We did, however, spend every moment of school time together. They taught me how to forge notes excusing me from school so we could go smoke cigarettes and shoplift. The Raggart sisters were blow job queens and dutifully tried to instruct me in practicing this fine art on enormous tubes of lip gloss that we ripped off from Woolworth's.

But while Rina and Rosie actually put all this into practice, giving assorted pimply youths what must have been the charge of their lives by taking turns blowing them, I was shy and geeky and just listened in wonder as they recounted their exploits. They lived with their mother in a trailer park on a mountain. While they, too, were a good ways from town, at least there were other kids around there. Kids to whom they eagerly taught the meaning of fun.

Once, I actually convinced Francine and Henry to let me spend a weekend at the Raggart residence. As we got off the school bus and walked down the dirt road to the trailer park, I felt free. The huge sky seemed less threatening here and the arridness of the earth now pleased me. Rina and Rosie had decided they were going to get me laid, and so we headed to the home of Paul, a blond burn-out with acne and a pinball machine in the basement. Paul came to the door and his dull face brightened as he presumed, I suppose, that this was yet another of his lucky days and the Raggarts were here to doubly fellate his pimply appendage.

"So, you guys wanna go down in the basement, play a little pinball or somethin'?" Paul drawled.

"Yes, but this is Zoe, you have to meet Zoe," Rosie said. I looked at Paul, Paul looked at me. He shrugged and led the way to the basement. As we descended into this tunnel of love, Rosie harshly whispered, "Act sexy, goddammit." I tried. But I didn't really have it in me. And Paul completely ignored me, leering instead at Rina, who was wearing a gingham skirt so short her white underpants peeked out the back. Soon, Paul had his hands up her skirt and had backed her against the pinball machine, where, with a combination come-here/get-away expression, Rina was exuding steaminess. Rosie got furious, though. "Paul, we're not here to blow you, we want you to *meet* Zoe. Rina, pull your skirt down." We all three guiltilly looked at Rosie. I didn't want Paul, Paul didn't want me. Rina wanted Paul and Paul wanted Rina and Rosie. Rosie was sick about it sensing a battle lost. She let Rina stay there with Paul and marched me out of the house.

"Zoe, you have to, you have to do it with somebody," she said, growing calmer, hoping perhaps to sink her point in with a gentler approach. I felt she was right: I did, indeed, have to *do it*. This, and only this, would perhaps break me of my maudlin chains of pubescent self-preoccupation and misery. I felt terrible about my obvious ineptitude as a thirteen-year-old seductress.

"We'll try Kenny," Rosie said then with a sigh.

"Oh, Rosie, do we have to?" I said. Rosie was shocked. And then took pity on me.

"Oh, all right, we'll just go to my house, I guess."

Rosie's mother was not at home but her older brother Ronnie was. I loved Ronnie at once. He was sixteen, a drop out, and gainfully employed as a gas station attendant in town. He was smeared in grease, that darkened his hair, which was red like the sisters'.

"Ronnie, this is Zoe, she's spending the weekend," Rosie announced, foraging for peanut butter and jelly in the kitchenette.

"Un," Ronnie grunted. He turned an eye on me, though, and I saw that eye linger. This was more like it. Rosie caught this, and as soon as Ronnie had left the room, said, "Why didn't I think of that! You can do it with Ronnie."

By evening, Rina was back from blowing Paul and she and Rosie connived to leave me alone with Ronnie in his room. After they left, we sat there awkwardly. I guess he had been given instruction because he said, "Come on, let's get in bed."

"Okay." I shrugged.

We lay side by side and stiff as boards. Ronnie, presumably, wasn't a virgin but he was incredibly tense right then. This made me tenser and soon we were both shaking. Then, off in the other room, the phone rang. Ronnie sprang up from the bed and raced out of the room. After a few minutes Rosie and Rina popped in.

"Well?" Rosie demanded.

"Well what?"

"What happened? Ronnie's gone. I hope you did it with him," said Rina.

"Where'd he go?" I asked.

"Over to his girlfriend's," Rosie said.

"Oh. No. We didn't do it."

"*Zoe,*" both Rosie and Rina said exasperatedly. But they gave up on the idea of getting me laid and after that we had a nice time smoking cigarettes, then went and got some pot from a fat hippie lady named Nellie, who lived down the road. Nellie was basically friendless and thirty and lured kids our age to sit with her for hours by getting them stoned. We got stoned and sat in the fat woman's trailer, being fed pot brownies and listening to hippie music.

About a year went by like this, living under the disdain of my parents and doing as much damage as possible when I could hang around with Rina and Rosie. One day it dawned on me that I did, after all, have a father, and whatever childhood allegiance I'd felt for my mother was long gone. I called Charlie, who hedged only slightly when I announced I was coming to live with him.

5

Satan's Closet

I am sitting in Satan's closet with a chain in my lap. Soon, he will come home and presumably get ready for bed. Once he is asleep, I will come out and chain him. I think it will be funny to chain him to his bed. I don't know if I'll actually leave him like that, chained up and helpless, but I might. If you think that it's going to be difficult for me, a petite woman, to chain him, a big devil, to his bed, you are wrong. Satan is on drugs. Every night at bedtime he pumps himself full of multicolored things to calm him and make him sleep. And sleep he does. Like a ship of bricks. Once, when we were still together,

I tried to wake him when I heard noise near the skylight and thought someone was trying to bust in and kill us. I shook Satan, called his name, pulled on his arm, all to no avail. Satan was profoundly out. Whatever or whoever was foraging near the skylight moved on, off to fossick elsewhere—but they could have shattered the glass, leapt down onto the bed, ripped off my limbs, and cooked me before Satan would have stirred.

But you know now I'm beginning to wonder, Why Satan? Why am I chaining *him* to a bed when it is Bev who I love best? Shouldn't I be hiding in *his* closet? Of course, Bev doesn't have a closet. He inhabits a tiny studio apartment in a remote corner of Brooklyn. He has more cockroaches than I do. But no closet for me to lurk in, waiting for him to come home so that I may chain him in and keep him there so that no one ever sleeps with him again.

Maybe I should pack my chain back up into its plastic garbage bag and go. Hail a cab. Over the bridge and into Brooklyn and land on Bev's doorstep. I don't have his keys anymore, though. But I could try to break in. He has a flimsy lock. What do you think? What's it going to be?

6

No One Is Anything
Next to You

When I first met Bev, the Hefty Lesbian whose name I can never remember was living directly upstairs from me. The first time that Bev and I lay in my loft bed touching each other's softest parts, Hefty was upstairs throwing couches at the wall. Bev and I could hear her rage; it made my ceiling shake. Hefty was, at that point, a recovering crack addict. This I knew because the building superintendent at that time, a guy named Dave, was also a recovering crack addict and apparently knew the Hefty Lesbian from NA or CA or Whatever A.

Dave has the longest dick I have ever seen in my life.

Once, my friend Jane and I were eating goat cheese salad at Mogador, a Moroccan restaurant we like, when Dave With the Long Dick walked in and sat down nearby.

Jane and I eat goat cheese salad at Mogador so often that all the waitresses know us. They know we order only two goat cheese salads and one piece of Chocolate Indulgence cake, but we tip well. The waitresses, therefore, are accommodating. The waitresses at Mogador are notoriously exotic and sexy. All the musicians I know discuss this fact. Almost all the musicians within a twenty-block radius of St. Marks Place eat at Mogador at least twice a week.

Once, one of the sexy Mogador waitresses was in a rock video of

Bev's band's song "Get This." For three hours one night I interrogated Bev as to whether or not he had flirted with the waitress from Mogador when she was in his video. He said he had not. She was not, he said, his type. And, more important, he said, he had me. This, of course, is what I wanted to hear. I don't know why he didn't know this all along. I don't know why I failed to communicate that I wanted to hear him say: I HAVE YOU I DON'T WANT THE WAITRESS FROM MOGADOR THEY ALL PALE NEXT TO YOU EVERY WOMAN I HAVE EVER KNOWN GOES PALE NEXT TO YOU NO ONE IS ANYTHING NEXT TO YOU. Finally he said it. We broke up anyway. Not over the waitress. I left him. I loved him, but still I left him.

I also left Dave with the incredibly long dick. Although technically, you'd have to say he left me. This was when the Hefty Lesbian Downstairs still lived upstairs.

So. Jane and I were eating goat cheese salad when Dave, former superintendent of my building and owner of an incredibly long dick, happened to walk in to Mogador. With him was a willowy blond woman. He is now married to her. I absolutely *hate* when men I've dated end up with willowy blondes or, for that matter, with anyone who does not look exactly like me. I am short, I am petite, I am certainly not willowy. My torso is long. My mother Francine's torso is also long and so is my half sister Louise's. We are Zoe, Louise, and Francine, the long-torsoed three. We all three like to swim and have a terrible time finding bathing suits that fit our long torsos. Thankfully, Francine found some long-torsoed suits in the Lands' End catalog five years ago. It is now a family tradition that every Christmas Francine gives me a Lands' End bathing suit. They are very durable suits, but I go through mine faster than Francine and Louise because I swim more often. I have time for that because I earn a living writing fuck books and screening dominatrixes phone calls, and these are not consuming professions. I have lots of time to swim.

When Dave walked into Mogador with his willowy blond girlfriend, he did not see me sitting there with Jane and the goat cheese salads brought to us by the waitress who was in Bev's rock video. The waitress does not know that Bev was my boyfriend. Because I am slightly perverse, I was tempted to ask her if she remembers whether the blond guy from the band Lotus Crew flirted with her. I'm not sure why I need this information. I'm not sure why my heart still hurts over someone I left. I'm not sure why my torso is so long.

Dave's long dick is not longer than my torso. That much I can tell you.

Dave and his blond girlfriend sat down two tables away from me and Jane. By then Jane and I were eating Chocolate Indulgence cake and Jane was speculating as to how many grams of fat were in the cake.

"I bet this cake isn't as fattening as avocados," I said.

Jane scoffed. I am always attacking her for eating avocados. My mother once told me avocados have lots of fat and I like to try convincing Jane that they have more fat than chocolate cake, I like to try to convince Jane that she is going to become a Big Fat Thing to whom no one will speak. She will grow so fat she will have no choice but to devote all her time to my needs. Her husband will still love her but be faintly repulsed by her jiggling bulk. He will be intrigued by the potential eroticism of fat but also will be worried about her emotional well-being. He will grow aloof and steely and she will come crawling to me, begging to tend to my every need.

But Jane just scoffed at my Avocados for Chocolate theory.

Then I said, "See that guy over there? He's got the longest dick I have ever seen in my life." I pointed discreetly toward Dave.

Jane's eyes came alive. "Really?" Jane is perverse. This is one reason I love her. She thrives on hearing about people with physical abnormalities and distresses. She particularly loves *my* distresses and/or humiliation caused by my bodily functions or those of people I know. Once, I ate an enormous number of dried apricots while on a train ride upstate with a new boyfriend. I hadn't eaten all day and so gorged on dried apricots. When we arrived at the boyfriend's grandparents' pristine cabin in the woods, I rushed into the bathroom because the apricot overdose was boiling down my intestinal tract. I will refrain from going into complete graphic illustration, but suffice it to say that on this, my fourth date with this very sweet and bordering-on-proper young man, I spent the better part of the weekend holed up in the toilet, squeezing out hideous, sulfuric-smelling goop. Because we didn't know each other very well, he made no comment at all. I was in the toilet at least once an hour and emerged with sulfuric shit smell clinging to my clothes, but he said nothing. In spite of this, I moved in with him a few months later. We lived together for two weeks and then I left him. I'm not sure if I loved him. If this whole sulfuric shit episode had happened with Bev, he would have asked me what the fuck was wrong with my bowels. Bev and I fell into that sort of intimacy right away. This is why I know I loved Bev. Of course, I left Bev for Satan. The first time I was at Satan's house, he walked in the bathroom while I was peeing. At first this shocked me but then I realized it really didn't bother me. I felt no physical embarrassment around Satan. None. Maybe this is why I left Bev for him. Or part of it.

This might be a good moment to weave in another story: Jane's husband, Martin, once shat in a plastic bag in a moving car.

(So did the Hefty Lesbian Downstairs. I know this because Dave With the Long Dick told me. He heard her tell the story during a self-help meeting.)

Martin and Jane were driving through Brooklyn with Martin's parents. Martin and Jane were in the backseat. At the time, they were junkies. They were respectable junkies, they had a home and they bathed regularly, but they were junkies all the same. Shitting, you may know, is very much disrupted by opiates. The foursome had just eaten a rich meal at a nice Brooklyn restaurant, and Martin's parents were now driving Martin and Jane back to Manhattan. Suddenly,

Martin's intestines seized up. "Mom, do you have a plastic bag up there?" he asked his mother. His mother continued to talk and handed him a plastic bag from the glove compartment. She did not ask her son, "Son, why the plastic bag?" She is not like that. Then, without his parents noticing, Martin wriggled his pants off his butt and discreetly shit into the plastic bag. He then carefully knotted it up and sat it at his feet. To this day I don't really understand *why* he didn't just ask them to pull over at a gas station. Maybe he is too fastidious for that. Better to shit in a car than at a gas station. I don't know. After a few minutes, the four of them were stopped at a light when Martin's father sniffed the air inside the car and said, "Does anyone else notice a strong odor of cheese?" Martin and Jane feigned ignorance, and when Martin's father rolled down the window to air out the cheese smell, Martin hurled the bag of shit out onto the Brooklyn-Queens Expressway.

You'll see that Martin and Jane are well matched. They take great pleasure in the descriptions of bodily functions and the rituals surrounding them.

And so, when I said, "That guy has the longest dick I've ever seen," Jane came to life.

"What do you mean? How long?" Her face twitched with curiosity and anticipation.

"You won't believe this, but at least a foot long and incredibly skinny. It was very uncomfortable," I said.

Jane giggled, then "Really?" she said. We both paused to look over at Dave. You would never guess it. He's not the kind of guy you look at and think, That guy's got the longest dick in the world. No. You would never suspect it. He's five foot ten, a hundred and fifty pounds, good face.

Dave rented me this apartment on Sixth Street five years ago. The one I'm sitting in right now. The one I moved to after I left the guy who pretended he didn't notice the sulfuric shit smell. I will never forgive him for that. I will never forgive him for not acknowledging all of me. He, in turn, will never forgive me for leaving him.

He still won't talk to me. Bev won't talk to me either. I am very upset about this. Other guys I left talk to me. Oliver the Bassoon Player talks to me. Oliver is now, as we know, one of my best friends. A best friend whom I frequently fondle on corners. Oliver is five foot nine, Caucasian, blue eyes. Oliver was the boyfriend before Bev, who was the boyfriend before Satan. It is a long trail of love.

I hate Bev for not talking to me. I hate him for not detailing to me his conquests, his hopes and fears, I hate him for not still calling me up and screaming, "YOU DUMPED ME." I hate that I still love Bev. I still love Oliver but that's different. I love Oliver because he is my friend. Because he *does* detail his sexual exploits to me. Because we are "guys" together. I like to have guy talk with guys even though I realize it is never truly genuine guy talk because I am a woman, and as much as Oliver pretends to tell me *all* the details of his and Bonnie's sex life, as much as he did in the past relay to me the details of tying Susan up and fucking her in the ass and two hours later racing off to not be late for a date with Meho the Japanese Art Student, who he would never tie up and with whom he did it strictly missionary style, as much as he purports to tell me everything, I know he does not. He holds out on me. He holds out because there remains a degree of sexual tension between us and there is also the idea that we ought to still be lovers since we do love each other but, because we are idiots, we find it difficult to be in love with those who love us.

I might add that Oliver and I are more physically comfortable together now than when we were actually intimate.

Now, back at Mogador, Jane began to hound me. "Come *on*, tell me about it," she said greedily.

"Oh, it was awful," I said, "I mean he took off his pants and I was shocked. It wasn't sexy, it was scary, like a pole, like I was an unwilling pole-vaulter."

"But then you fucked?"

"Well yeah, sort of. But it was like a needle or something, it was really uncomfortable. I didn't not come. We did it and then I went home. He lived downstairs from me. He was the super."

"You fucked your super?" She practically choked, visualizing perhaps her own potbellied super, whose hands, she had once told me in exacting detail, were subject to horrific dermatitis.

"Well, he's not the super now. And look at him. I mean he's cute, he doesn't *look* like a super."

She obediently glanced in his direction again. "So, *how* long?" she asked. "*This* long?" She extended her hands the length of the table.

"No, I'd say *this* long," I said, extending my own hands the width of the table. We both cackled.

Jane wanted to know more about Dave's long dick. I told her as much as I could remember, which was not very much. I felt acutely uncomfortable with Dave. He's the kind of guy who would have completely ignored a sulfuric shit smell. In fact, I could have shit on his *head* and he would have pretended it didn't happen because he wouldn't have been comfortable with my bodily functions or anyone else's. As it happened, he never called me again after I saw his incredibly long dick. Which technically means he dumped me. But I had mentally dumped him before we even had sex. It was absolutely a fluke that I *did* have sex with him after what he put me through.

On our first and only date, Dave stood there, in his apartment, playing guitar really loudly. We'd had a cheap greasy dinner, then he'd insisted we go back to his place, which was two flights down from my own. His apartment had no life. Things were methodical. Not particularly clean, just dully methodical. As I took this in, Dave plugged in his Les Paul and started to play. I didn't know what he was thinking. That this was appealing? I then sat through TWO HOURS of BUSY BLUES LICKS. Obviously, I am an imbecile to have sat through such a thing. Or maybe just pathetically insecure. I kept thinking, If I don't keep sitting here, he will be offended and I can't offend him.

I want people to like me. I wish I didn't. A lot of things go wrong when we want people to like us. We lose the serrated edge that attracts them to us in the first place. We sit through bad blues licks. We crumble, we fall, we tether ourselves to infinite failability.

When Dave finally stopped playing guitar, I was a speechless and exhausted idiot. I wanted to melt into the nasty little couch, to become one with its synthetic tendrils. And then Dave kissed me.

I don't know why or how, but we were soon naked on his narrow bed. What came to mind at that moment was my little sister Louise's way of saying "I can't believe this is *actually* happening." One day she just started saying "I can't believe this is *actually* happening" in a monotone drawl. She would sometimes alternate this with "Could you please pass the jelly?" Drawling out the "jelly" to give it three syllables. Anything you said to Louise was met with "I can't believe this is *actually* happening. Or could you please pass the jelly?"

This was what I thought of then, as Dave's pole dick stood at full attention, ready to poke: I Can't Believe This Is Actually Happening. Then we were going at it: Could You Please Pass the Jelly? Going at it very uncomfortably, I might add: I Can't Believe This Is Actually Happening. Neither one of us came, and after trying awhile, we both lay there, not touching. Finally, I put on my clothes, mumbled some postcoital something, and went back to my hovel.

After this, if Dave and I happened to run into each other in the hall, we exchanged artificially bright hellos and kept going, glad the other didn't want to talk or, worse yet, have another go at it.

This whole thing was really Ravi's fault. He was the guy who ignored my apricot shit smell. Or, actually, maybe it was my fault for *moving in* with someone who ignored my sulfuric shit smell.

I gave up my apartment to move in with Ravi. We had seven blissful days of shacking up, then, on the eighth day, I started to feel nauseous whenever he was within a few feet of me. I didn't yet understand the twisted dichotomy of emotional idiocy. I didn't know that Repulsion is part of the game and is the most intimate partner of Attraction. And so when Repulsion came, I left. Ravi screamed but I didn't scream back. Eventually, he went cold and I packed my stuff up.

I went looking for an apartment. Which brings us back to Dave With the Long Dick. He rented me the apartment where I still live.

Now Dave is married to a willowy blonde. Presumably her willowiness allows for a genital construction that is conducive to Dave's long dick. He was not married to her when Jane and I saw him at Mogador. He married her a few months later. I know this because the Hefty Lesbian Downstairs told me so. I didn't ask, she just told me. She talks too much. Which is probably why I don't remember her name. I hate when people talk too much.

When I first lived here, the Hefty Lesbian lived above me. Next to the Heavy Metal Guitarist. The Hefty Lesbian lived with her girlfriend. They were both recovering crack addicts. The girlfriend's name was Alison. I remember this because Alison was likable. She did not talk all the time.

One day, Alison and the Hefty Lesbian moved out. I was coming back from the vet with Wimpy in his cat carrier. The vet's name was Dr. Mary Toe. She had fondled Wimpy's huge belly, while I'd noted the extraordinarily long black hairs on her forearms.

"Well, the big guy seems to be fine," Dr. Mary Toe said.

"What?" She'd startled me. I was wondering what the length and density of her arm hair boded about the rest of her body hair. Did she have a pubic forest? And how did her husband, Dr. Portnoy, the other vet in the practice, negotiate this forest?

"Wimpy is fine," Dr. Toe said again.

"Oh, good." I smiled and packed Wimpy back up into the cat carrier. I said good-bye to the hairy vet and headed home.

When I walked into the hallway, I saw that Alison and Hefty and Dave With the Long Dick were moving Alison and Hefty's belongings out. They all stopped to stare into the cat carrier. Hefty said, "What happened, that cat ate the Bronx?" Then she laughed a horrible wheezing laugh. I ha-ha-ha'd at her, then walked on down the hall. I never asked where they were going or why. I didn't care. Although Alison was bearable, I would never tell her my problems.

Not too long after that, Dave also moved out. Once, I ran into him on the street. This was right after I'd made a television appearance with SLANG, the all-girl band I was in. Our songs had titles like "STICK THAT IN YOUR LAUGH HOLE" and "MY BOYFRIEND MADE ME BULEMIC." We were lazy and not very talented, but we did manage to make a CD and one TV appearance the *Mark Bronson Show*, a late-night talk show hosted by a guy who was a dead ringer for Truman Capote in his bloated period. A show that Dave With the Long Dick had apparently tuned in to, for when I ran into him on the street, I could see a self-impressed look in his eyes: He had put his incredibly long dick inside of someone who was on television.

Coincidentally, Bev, whom I hadn't met yet, had also tuned in to this show. As Dave With the Long Dick was sitting in front of his TV, musing about our shared past, so was Bev musing that he might be inclined to see me, the person on TV, naked.

Another coincidence was that the first and last time our band was treated to a plush lunch by the record company, a weasly A&R guy named Herb invited me to come with him and see a band called Lotus Crew that night at CBGB's. I thought ingratiating myself to the guy might help my own band's cause and keep me from going back to a real job. So I went to CBGB's with Herb, the weasely A&R guy.

The club was choked with people, record executives with small eyes, young girls with itty-bitty backpacks, bitter musicians, hopeful young musicians, and secretaries with pierced nostrils. Lotus Crew had started already. They were actually good. They were causing this cluster of sweaty white people to try to dance. White people dancing can be embarrassing. Like heavy petting with someone you've known for many years and never thought of in sexual terms. Suddenly, your hand is down his pants. You fit your paw around his appendage, you look into his face and see that it is the face of your friend Buddy, for whom you never had sexual feelings. And now, for some unfathomable reason, your hand is down his pants and you are profoundly embarrassed. This band, then, would make putting your hand down your friend Buddy's pants seem perfectly natural.

This band was good enough to make its fans seem graceful when they danced.

The singer was a lanky blond boy in a white T-shirt. He looked like a sexy rubber band. He wore glasses that kept getting jolted to the end of his nose. As Herb the Weasel, now grossly drunk, started breathing on my neck, I felt a budding desire to adjust the singer's glasses. Or to perhaps hold his glasses for him while he played. As I envisioned this, me, standing, holding the blond guy's glasses, Herb, trying to whisper something at me, drooled on my neck. Just then the band stopped playing and the singer said, "Thank you, get home safely, never drive a car when you're dead." He stepped off the stage and walked past me. And as Herb turned to drool on a cocktail waitress, I headed toward the exit.

The singer was standing near the door, talking to two girls who, from the looks of things, were also determined to hold his glasses. The girls were ugly and had nasal voices. I hadn't planned on talking to the singer but was overcome with the injustice of it: nasal girls talking to a guy whose glasses I wanted to hold. I stopped, looked at the singer, and said, "Do you have a quarter?"

This shut the girls up and appeared to please the singer. He pushed his glasses back, beamed at me, and said, "Yes! I do!" as if he had been waiting for this request most of his adult life. He started to dig around in his pockets. I saw a gap between his front teeth. Not quite big enough to stick the tip of one's tongue into, too big to trap unsightly bits of food. In that instant I realized two things: that he had the quintessentially perfect gap between his teeth and that I would probably love him very soon. He produced a quarter and put it in my hand. The room shifted as this happened. The Nasal Girls were getting smaller and smaller, as if shrinking themselves to fit into the itty-bitty backpacks they were wearing. The singer's glasses rode once more down his nose. I reached up and very gently pushed them back to the top of his nose.

"Thank you," he said.

"Anytime," I said.

41

"Really?" he said.

"Oh yes," I said. We grinned like imbeciles. "I'm Zoe," I said.

"Oh, I know," he said.

"You do?"

"I saw you on TV."

"You did?"

"Yeah. I watch the *Mark Bronson Show* all the time. I love that guy. He looks like Truman Capote on his deathbed."

"You're kidding."

"No, really, he does."

"No, I mean, I *know* he does. But no one else sees the resemblance.

"Oh, it's obvious. People have difficulty seeing the obvious. My name is Bev."

"What?"

"B–E–V."

"Really?"

"Why?" he said, slightly defensive, as if maybe he'd been tortured and pummeled over this name in grade school.

"That's one of the twins in *Dead Ringers*," I said.

"What's that?"

"Oh, it's a great movie about twin gynecologists. Their identities get increasingly blurred as they descend into addiction and end up performing surgery on each other and dying."

"Cool."

"Well, yeah. I have brothers who are twins. I always try to get them to watch it because they seem to deny their twinness. I'm fascinated by it. You know?"

"I do, " he said. And I firmly believed that he did.

"Hey, Zoe," he said then, "can I have my quarter back?"

"Oh," I said, forlorn. "Here." I gave him the quarter.

"I want to call you and see if you'll go to the movies with me."

"Oh," I said, relieved.

We walked to the sweaty phone booth at the other end of the club. I dialed my number and handed him the receiver. He talked to my machine. "Hi, Zoe, this is Bev, like *Dead Ringers*. I met you a few minutes ago. I'm wondering if you'd like to go to the movies. My number is 718 555-0044. Give me a call." As he hung up the phone, a hand reached in and grabbed hold of his shoulder.

"Young man, come with me," a guy said.

Bev and I both turned around, startled.

"Yes, sir," Bev said then, nodding at a short swarthy guy who was still holding him by the shoulder.

"This is my manager, Carlton," Bev said then. "I think he wants me to go ingratiate myself to strangers now. It was an honor to meet you, Zoe." Bev extended his hand then and we shook. As we did this, his glasses rode down his nose again.

Carlton led Bev away.

The next night, we went to see the movie *Ed Wood*. Bev laughed a lot. At things no one else laughed at. This I liked. That he found humor in unusual places. Also, I liked the laugh itself. It was completely unguarded.

Afterward, he walked me home and we kissed while standing on the stoop of my building. This kiss at first light, tender, then probing, deeper, nearly menacing.

The Hefty Lesbian appeared about two minutes into the kiss. She wasn't living in the building at the time. Maybe she was there borrowing money from the Heavy Metal Guitarist. I don't know. But she was in a foul mood and, because Bev and I were blocking her way, said, "Take that shit inside, man."

We didn't, though. We were, after this kiss and after the Hefty Lesbian's dose of bitterness, very shy.

"So. Now what?" Bev said when we parted lips.

"Er . . ." I demurred. What "Now what"? What? Rip each other's clothes off? On the street? Upstairs? Did he want to come up? Should he?

"No, I didn't mean should I come up, I meant I'm going on the road tomorrow."

"Oh, right. I'm going, too. Day after tomorrow," I said then. "It's our last gasp. If we don't break even, we're breaking up. I'll go back to my, uh . . . receptionist job."

"You should get paid to *exist*," Bev said. "When are you coming back?"

"Two weeks. You?"

"Same."

"Wow. Well."

"Two weeks, then? We'll go bowling?"

"Bowling?"

"Yeah. I bowl well. People fall in love with me when I bowl."

"Oh." This a dejected "Oh," an "Oh" envisioning droves of girls with pierced nostrils watching Bev bowl. Swooning over Bev's bowling.

"It' s a joke, I'm joking, no one falls in love with me when I bowl, I swear, I don't have a million girls sending me bowling baubles, really."

"Oh. Bowling baubles?"

"Bowling baubles," he said. We kissed again. The Hefty Lesbian came back out. She was on a rampage. She glowered at us. We separated lips. He backed away from me slowly, then turned and walked away.

By Day 5 of the two weeks, we had left each other thirty-seven messages on our home machines. When, on Day 8, Slang played in Rochester on the night that Lotus Crew played in Buffalo, Bev coerced his roadie, Pete, into driving him to Rochester at two A.M. to visit my humble Days Inn room.

It was nearly four A.M. when Pete the Roadie dropped Bev off. The Days Inn receptionist must have been suspicious of Bev and his ill-fitting pants. She rang my room and dubiously asked, "Are you expecting a Bev?" I said I was expecting a Bev.

I opened the door to my Days Inn room and there stood Bev. He was carrying a doctor's bag, his idea of a suitcase. His glasses were at the edge of his nose. He looked like a precocious medical student.

"It's you," I said. We kissed.

While Bev and I stood kissing in the doorway to Room 115, the

Hefty Lesbian was presumably safely asleep somewhere in Manhattan. Dave With the Long Dick was perhaps on his honeymoon with the willowy blonde. Jane was probably asleep. The waitress from Mogador was maybe on an incredibly long rock video shoot. It was going all night. And she had to be at Mogador to waitress the next morning.

I took Bev's hand and led him into the room. We sat on my bed. I touched his arm. He had blond hairs on his arm. I have brown hairs on my arms. Not so many, though. I don't have hairy arms. Satan, predictably, has black hairs on his arms. Like Dr. Mary Toe. But I didn't know Satan yet. This was still the paradise before the purgatory.

I was kissing Bev, deliciously kissing Bev. We learned the shapes of each other's bodies. Although not every shape. If Bev had had an abnormally long dick, I would not have found it out that night.

As it happens, he does not. There is nothing abnormal about Bev's dick. This I learned on our third date.

Now, on our second date, at the Days Inn, on the narrow bed in a room with green carpeting and orange curtains, as we touched parts of each other, the TV was on in the background. It was tuned to an HBO movie with a light-jazz soundtrack. I said, "Bev, I have to tell you something."

"Yes?" he said, his clear blue eyes open and frank and yet worried that I was about to make some terrible pronouncement.

"I absolutely hate light jazz."

This, Bev later said, was what made him feel compelled to love me. That I thought it might be a problem that I hated light jazz. That I realized we might have different taste in music and, conceivably, his taste allowed for light jazz and I was already worrying he might hope I would listen to light-jazz records with him at some future date when we were holed up in his or my apartment, fucking and laughing. This is when he loved me.

After I left Bev for Satan, Bev and his band went to play in France. One night, he met a girl who took him home and gave him some heroin. He liked it a lot. He liked the girl, too. I knew this because he refused to detail his night with her for me. Bev refused to tell me about the heroin girl in France, because I had just broken up with him, because I was going to Rome for a week with Satan, because Satan didn't mind if I read detective novels shortly after we fucked because he, too, read things after we fucked. We fucked and we read. Bev had demanded that I pay attention to him for two hours after fucking. I should not want to read Andrew Vachss after sex. This, he thought, demeaned the way our bodies and spirits had entwined. It did not. It just meant that I have only a certain tolerance for staring into people's eyes. After a while, I need to read about murder. I loved Bev impossibly but could only demonstrate this in brief spurts interspersed with murder. People have different tolerance levels. This is a factor in compatability. I could not maintain Bev's pace and, while he was on the road, I met someone whose pace was the same as mine. Which should have raised the first red flag. But it didn't. And now Bev wouldn't detail his night with French Heroin Girl for me. She, I'm sure, did not want to read after sex. She probably asked him to autograph her Lotus Crew CD and he probably did.

But that was all when Bev still talked to me. That was before the Hefty Lesbian moved back in. She moved out and then, a few months later, she moved back in. Without her girlfriend.

She took the worst apartment in the building. The one on the ground floor facing the street. Loud. Dangerous because kids throw things at the windows. Dave had something to do with her moving back here. He's not the super anymore but he still has pull with the owner. He used his pull to help the Hefty Lesbian, who was on the pipe again. As it turns out, moving back here didn't help her keep off the pipe. I saw her smoking crack in the hall. I think she was doing it in the hall because by then she had a new girlfriend who was living with her. A very quiet girl. Very small and never said a word. Built somewhat like me. Like maybe she has a long torso.

The Hefty Lesbian did not know I saw her smoking crack. She thought she'd put her pipe away before I noticed. She thought you couldn't still smell it or see the little pale cloud of what came out of her lungs.

I got my mail out of the box and Hefty said, "Dave got married."

"Oh yeah?"

"Yeah, to that blond girl. You saw her. She lived here with him back when I still lived upstairs."

"Oh yeah, I guess."

And then she said, "Dave's got a really long dick, doesn't he?"

Now she totally had me. She had said something that required my attention. She had said something that required me to stop marginalizing her as a bigmouthed fat crackhead lesbian. She had acknowledged that she knew that I knew that Dave had an abnormally long dick.

"Yeah," I said after a pause, "he really does."

We smiled at each other then. I didn't ask her how *she*, a lesbian, knew about Dave's dick. Sometimes lesbians sleep with men. Sometimes lesbians who sleep with men are marginalized by lesbians who don't sleep with men. And the reverse is also true. No one is very tolerant. We're just not made that way.

In Rome, Satan showed me Caravaggio. I left Bev shortly after I met Satan. I didn't want to leave Bev but I had to be with Satan. I don't know why. To this day I can offer no explanation for it. But I had to do it. I had to leave Bev, whom I loved. Satan was familiar, Satan was like me, and this, although predictable, was more comfortable.

Satan and I met in a deli. Satan was in the deli with Chris the Ugly Philosopher, a guy I knew marginally but didn't much like. Ugly Chris was buying beer. Chris is not physically ugly. He is just ugly. An academic who likes to slum by drinking a lot of beer, eating burgers, and picking up strippers and waitresses. I knew this because he had once dated Daisy the Fading Stripper from my building. He had treated her cruelly. She had gone on Prozac shortly afterward.

Chris, then, was buying beer. I was buying fruit.

"Hey, Zoe, how's it going?" Chris said, clutching a six-pack.

"Oh, hi, Chris," I said.

"Zoe, this is Jackson." Ugly Chris introduced his friend. He was strange looking. His hair was too long and his eyes were a hard and violent green. Still, he was beautiful.

"Hi," I said flatly. I turned back to fondling melons.

"No, that's not a good one," Jackson said, taking the fruit right out of my hands. "Here," he said, picking a different melon, "this one should be perfect." I shrugged. He smiled then. His smile was wicked and beautiful. It lit his face and invited me in. He followed me home from the deli. Which I didn't know till I reached my stoop. Then, as Mikey the Heavy Metal Guitarist came crashing out the front door, bumping his amplifier down the steps, I turned around and saw Jackson.

"Oh . . ." I said.

"I hope you don't mind being stalked. Would you like to have dinner?"

"Uh . . ."

"Oh, good. Here's my phone number, call me later." He handed me a card, turned, and walked away.

We had dinner the next night.

Bev was on the road. But Bev was never stupid. It did not take long for him to put it together. The night after I had dinner with Satan, Bev E-mailed a note saying, *Please, Zoe, just don't fuck anyone before I get home, okay? I mean, while I'm home would be equally depressing, but wait, just wait.*

Satan and I had dinner twice more and then, one night, I went home with him. Ostensibly just to look at his artwork. As I gawked with curiosity at his sculptures, I said, "Oh, I think my boyfriend would like these." Satan put his hands on my shoulders and kissed me. Then it was all over.

The next night, when I talked to Bev, he was in Indianapolis.

"You weren't home last night. I tried to call all night." His voice was flat.

"I'm sorry, Bev."

"Zoe, this is really deeply fucking depressing. What if I fucked some underage honeydip from the front row in Indianapolis tonight, what would you think? What if I found somebody I actually liked? I realize you're not exactly Commitment Girl—I've realized this since the moment I met you. Maybe this is you coming to the realization that this thing with me is serious shit."

"I know that, Bev. I want it to be serious shit. I'm confused, though."

"What's his name?"

Two nights later, Detroit:

"Hi, Bev."

"Oh, Zoe, I didn't think you'd call. I'm scared."

"Me, too."

"There's this note in your voice I haven't heard before. It scares me."

"But I love you."

"Yeah. And I'm not there. And *Satan* is."

"Satan?"

"Satan. Whatever his name is."

"Jackson."

"*Jack*-son? You're fucking a guy named Jackson? I'm in *Detroit* and you're fucking a guy named *Jackson*?"

Chicago:

"Zoe, tell me what you want. If you want to work this out, I have to know. For real."

"I do, but I don't know."

"You're jerking me around. Okay. You fucked someone. Let's move on."

"I can't."

"Can't what?"

"I just can't. Move on. I don't know."

* * *

Montreal:

"Hi, Bev, it's me."

"Now what."

"I don't like what's happening."

"Oh, and I do? I'm out here sleeping in a Days Inns and you're fucking the devil. Fine. Fuck the devil. Then come back. But you just keep telling me you're confused. I don't know what that means. I wish you'd just spout out a torrent of emotions so I could know what all the conflicting ones are. I wish you could communicate."

"I'm trying."

"I feel like one of those idiotic songs where the singer is saying, 'No, no, look, look how much I love you. Can you see? Look. I love you so much it's scientifically impossible for you not to love me back. Look. See? Look. See?' "

And I did love him back. And yet when, two weeks after I'd met him, Satan had to go to Rome to take care of sculptor business, I went with him. I broke up with Bev and went to Rome with Satan. We stayed in a villa up on a hill. We tooled around on a Vespa. We fucked. We read. We stood hand in hand in little churches where the Caravaggios hung, off in dark corners, lit by electric light boxes that you pumped coins into. I thought of Bev. As I stood, my hand in Satan's, my hand comfortable in Satan's, I thought of Bev, flailing through an endless series of Days Inns and underage girls. I dreamt of Bev. As Satan lay one night, zonked out on the antipanic medication he had to take in order to sleep, I dreamt I was choking. In the dream, I kept trying to wake Satan; I shook him, I pummeled his face with my fists, but he wouldn'd wake up and perform the Heimlich maneuver. In the dream, I knew I would have to crawl to the phone and call Bev in order to be saved. But I couldn't. I couldn't move off the bed and I couldn't wake Satan. When I finally came out of the dream, bathed in sweat, I ran into the other room and called Bev. He was not at home, of course. He was somewhere on the road and I didn't know where. I got scared. And it was too late.

Jane and I had now finished our meal. We paid the bill, leaving a generous tip for the waitress, who had been in Bev's rock video. Dave and the willowy blonde were still sitting there. They had long finished eating but were gazing into each other's eyes. Jane and I both glanced in the direction of Dave's crotch, but there was no evidence of the long dick. We walked outside to where Jane had chained her bike to a lamppost. We kissed each other's cheeks. Jane rode away and I walked home.

Daisy the Fading Stripper was sitting on the building stoop crying. The Hefty Lesbian was standing over her, speaking in soothing tones. I brushed by them and let myself in the building.

Jane and I were together one other time when we ran into Dave With the Long Dick. We were going to see Bev's band play. Jane was with me because I was, by then, involved with Satan, but neither Jane nor I really trusted me to simply go hear Bev's band and not talk to Bev and not go have coffee with Bev and not stay with Bev all night if that's how long it took for him to say he missed me and no one is anything next to me. So Jane came with me even though my half sister, Louise, was visiting for the weekend and it was Louise who really wanted to see Bev's band in the first place. Louise is only nineteen and could therefore not be trusted to remind me not to flirt with my ex-boyfriend and jeopardize my relationship with Satan. So Jane came with me and Louise even though she had to get up early to go to yoga.

Oliver the Basson Player also goes to Jane's yoga class. He and Jane see each other there. Jane likes Oliver because he always smiles as if he's just swallowed a naughty secret. She also likes him because she knows I love him, and she and I have been friends for fourteen years.

Jane and I met at a heroin dealer's house. Now we don't do heroin. We obsess over grams of fat and things that are wrong with people's bodies. Ours is the most enduring friendship either of us has. So when I love someone, usually Jane at least likes them. The reverse is also true.

Jane and Louise and I walked into the club. It was incredibly crowded. Bev's band had grown in popularity. I hated this because it was why Bev was away all the time. Thousands of people wanted to watch him play things. If he hadn't been away all the time, I would not have gone to dinner with Satan.

Two things happened when Jane and Louise and I walked into the club to see Bev and Lotus Crew play. First, we saw Dave With the Long Dick standing at the bar with his willowy blond wife. I reminded Jane, "That's the guy with the incredibly long dick." Then I said, "Oh, hi, Dave," when he saw me. Then I had to tell Louise the story of Dave's dick. I told her that it was practically as long as our torsos. We wondered if our mother had ever seen a dick nearly as long as our torsos. We decided it was unlikely but we know nothing about our mother's sex life because our mother is incredibly circumspect about everything.

Then we all saw Bev. He was getting ready to walk to the stage. His band mates all said hello to me and looked a little nervous. Bev himself was hard to read. If seeing me made his wounds hurt, he wasn't letting on. We didn't talk. We hugged each other.

Then Bev went on the stage and played things. He was tall, he was blond, he was playing things. He had fucked French girls who gave him heroin. He hadn't let me read in bed. I loved him. Yet I was with someone else.

Dave With the Long Dick looked at Bev. Dave's willowy wife looked at Bev. Jane and I and my long-torsoed sister Louise looked at Bev.

Satan was in France for two weeks. Showing people things he had sculpted.

The Hefty Lesbian was in detox.

When Bev and his band finished playing, Jane and Louise and I walked home. Jane and Louise did not ask how it felt to see Bev and I did not volunteer it. It felt awful. My wounds hurt. But in a few days Satan would be back. Things with Satan were, at that point, simple. We understood each other. He let me read after we fucked. He did not grope for parts of me I did not know how to expose.

When Satan came back from France, he told me he had had a bad experience with apricots. He had eaten only two apricots, not even dried ones, real live apricots, and he'd had diarrhea for days. This he told me without even knowing my own apricot story. It was then that I told him my own apricot story. He swore he would ask me what was wrong if I had a sulfuric shit smell clinging to me. I believed him. I trusted him.

By the time the Hefty Lesbian came back from detox, her girl-friend had left her. This I knew because I heard her telling it to the Heavy Metal Guitarist. I suppose that, theoretically, the Hefty Lesbian is now a recovering crackhead again. She is not actively a crackhead.

But I still don't know what her name is.

7

Why?

I am drooling now. I briefly fell asleep here in Satan's closet. A little bit of spittle got on my sweater. This is not good. I have to look my best when I chain Satan to his bed. Where is he? And where is Bev? Is he at home in Brooklyn? Should I go over there? Would he talk to me if I chained him to his bed? Would he detail his hopes and fears? Why is Satan so late getting home? Why did he leave me? Why did I leave Bev? Who am I?

8

Geek Love

Francine and Henry weren't sorry to see me go. I didn't know how life with Charlie was going to be, but it had to be better than it had been with Francine and Henry.

Charlie's girlfriend, Pansy, met me at the Baltimore airport. Yes, Charlie was the kind of guy to shack up with a girl named Pansy. And I am the kind of girl to call people I loved Satan.

Pansy's name did not suit her at all. She was a tiny dark-haired Jewish woman from a rich family, a family that did not approve of her shacking up with Charlie, but Pansy was a strong-willed thing, and at that point, her will seemed to be to marry Charlie. To this end, she had volunteered to come get me at the airport.

I deplaned and Pansy, recognizing me from a snapshot Charlie had given her, approached. "Hi, you must be Charlie's daughter. I'm Pansy and this is Honey," she said, presenting a rat-sized dog. The dog yapped at me. Pansy helped with my luggage and we got into her small expensive car and drove into the netherregions of Maryland.

Pansy and I didn't say much to each other during the drive, and after two hours, we pulled up to a quaint white clapboard farmhouse.

"Your father isn't here right now, but go in the house, Molly will show you where to put your stuff," Pansy said. Molly was, as Pansy had disapprovingly told me, the girl who was working for Charlie.

Charlie, whose career was endlessly up and down, was now up and was running his own horse farm as opposed to working for a rich guy. Molly, his hireling, I surmised, was attractive, because it didn't sound as though Pansy liked her.

"I've got to go muck some stalls now, but I'll see you later," Pansy said, then called to Honey the Rat Dog, who yapped and followed Pansy into the barn.

One of my father's great pleasures in life was getting his rich girlfriends to perform menial tasks while the hired help took it easy. Which is why Pansy was going to shovel shit while Molly was in the house arranging things. I hauled my duffel bags in through the front door and a tall blond woman wrapped her arms around me and said, "Hey, you're Zoe," as if I were her long-lost best friend.

I wasn't used to any kind of demonstrativeness. I pulled back. This didn't phase Molly.

"Your dad went to town to get some groceries, but he'll be back soon. He's real excited you're gonna be living here. We all are."

A little while later, Charlie came home, bearing bundles of groceries, and as Molly unpacked these, Charlie hugged me hello. "Hey, daughter, you're here," he said. There was an awkward pause and then he showed me around the house.

My room was small and quaint, with wood floors and a narrow bed, which was already made up. I imagined he'd had the reluctant Pansy perform this bed-making task. There was also a chest of drawers and a TV. I parked in front of the thing. Charlie cleared his throat a few times to get my attention but I was transfixed.

"Didn't they let you watch TV?"

"Oh no, we didn't have one," I said, flipping through the channels. Charlie shook his head, then said dinner would be in a half hour. I heard the heels of his cowboy boots clack softly as he went down the stairs and back into the kitchen.

When I came down, Charlie was flipping steaks. The smell of his cologne mixed with that of the meat. Molly was arranging places at the table and Pansy was presumably still in the barn, doing the menial work.

When we sat down to dinner, Charlie at one end of the table, Pansy at the other, me and Molly on the sides, I noticed that Charlie could barely eat for watching Molly's every move. Charlie was after Molly and this was not lost on Pansy, who ate in mincingly small bites, shoving food past her tight narrow lips as if she were being force-fed.

After a few days, I settled into a routine of sorts, going to junior high school by day and hanging around Molly by night. Charlie was always up to something. Either he and Pansy were holed up in his bedroom or he was out in the barn. Charlie was incredibly fastidious about the upkeep of the barn and the horses and everything sparkled and fell into perfect place. He ordered his exterior universe because he could not quite organize his internal life. He didn't seem to know exactly what to do with me, his suddenly acquired daughter. He meant well, but he was at a loss.

No one had time to drive me an hour to the nearest town for ballet lessons, my ballet career ended, and I discovered music. Molly had two Patti Smith records that I listened to obsessively. I also met a fevered budding rock chick who lived within walking distance of our farm. Her name was Sherri Panowitz, she was fifteen, had streaked hair and played bass. We'd hole up in her room, smoking pot and listening to Kiss and Ted Nugent. Sherri's mom was incredibly young— she'd had Sherri at sixteen—and she was very easygoing. She'd come home from her job at the beauty parlor and knock on Sherri's bedroom door. She'd be greeted by a cloud of pot smoke, some Kiss power chords, and two red-eyed stoner chicks. "Oh, hello, girls, just checking that you're alive in here. Why don't you come into the kitchen and talk to me a minute."

We'd reluctantly get up from where we were lying, zombielike, on the floor.

She would make us sandwiches and try to fix our hair. She was

as that made us look like sluts. We
's mom thought that this androg-
the road to dykedom. I think she
om unexpectedly to try catching us
s. At fifteen, though, any homo feelings
e appalling to us, and we certainly weren't
other to the strains of "I Want to Rock 'n' Roll

y boy I got close to at this point was Billy the Hay
Guy. He was basically a backwoods sub-dwarf but, all the
, one day when he was hurling bales of hay into the hayloft, I
went up there and sort of shimmied around while he worked. Then, without a word, he pushed me back onto a bale and began kissing me. I started wondering if maybe we were going to actually fuck, something I hadn't yet done, but then, as I fiddled with his belt, he said, "I love you, Zoe," and I freaked out.

I felt nauseous. I don't think I said one more word to him. I adjusted my clothing and climbed down from the hayloft. From then on, if and when the poor guy set foot on our farm, I ignored him.

After a few months, Charlie's luck changed for the worse and we packed up and moved to Upstate New York, where he'd been offered a job managing a rich guy's stable. We hadn't been in Maryland long, so, other than Sherri, I had no friends to leave behind. Then Molly announced she was going back to her native Georgia. This devastated both Charlie and me.

Molly helped us pack up and then, as Charlie and I headed north, she headed south. In New York Charlie really cleaned his slate. He broke up with Pansy and acquired not one but two girlfriends. The weekend girlfriend was Amy and Amy was a powerhouse. She lived in Manhattan and worked as a television producer. She would frequently whisk me off for days at a time, bringing me to the city, where she'd buy me clothes and take me to places like Studio 54. One night at Studio 54 I found myself in a corner, making out with some

tattered waitresses with names like Delilah and Tammy served us grilled cheese sandwiches and French fries and flirted with Charlie. These fifteen-minute flirt sessions seemed to sustain him and he'd walk out of those diners with a big grin, then get back in the cab of the truck and put on some George Jones and drive.

Georgia was a big shock. By now I had blue hair and loved the Sex Pistols. I wore dog collars. As we pulled in the driveway to Redwood Farms, our new home, Charlie said, "Zoe, you take off that dog collar or I'm sending you back to your mom and that geek she's married to."

I removed the dog collar and even agreed to put on a baseball cap. We got out of the truck and went to look for the owner of the farm, Charlie's new boss, Mr. Thompson. Thompson lived in a big white mansion at the end of the property. We knocked on the door and were greeted by a black maid. Things like race had never really occurred to me till that moment, seeing this black woman in a stupid outfit, actually *curtsying* as she ushered us in. I pulled my baseball cap farther down over my blue head. Now three matching redheads in designer jeans descended a *Gone With the Wind* staircase. With them was a tall white man. He was white all over. Hair, skin, clothes. This was Mr. Thompson. The redheads were his daughters. Snotty little things, each pudgier and beadier-eyed than the next. I guess I was expected to *mingle* as Thompson whisked Charlie off into an office to talk business. All I could do, though, was stare from them to the black woman, who was now dusting. I really couldn't think of anything to say. Then, one of them, who was probably my age, said, "Are you gwana be goin' ta Pinetop Academy?"

"Uh, I don't know," I said.

"Well, ya haveta, ya know. The public school's jus' nothin' but tha undesirable element."

"Ah." Later I learned this meant black people went to the public school.

All the same, Charlie insisted I attend Pinetop Academy. We

settled into a little postage-stamp house at the other end of the property and Charlie carted me off to enroll at Pinetop. Which was a disaster. I had never been the poster child for popularity, but now I was outright ostracized. Even the teachers were afraid of me. There were apparently no burn-outs. No one even smoked cigarettes. They all wore alligator shirts and designer jeans. And listened to disco.

Fortunately, a few things happened. One was that Molly, who'd been living in nearby Augusta, came to work with Charlie. She moved into a trailer a little ways down the road from us. She was in love now, with a jockey named Clyde, who was a foot shorter than her. She spent a lot of time with Clyde but often let me come over to loaf on the couch and listen to Patti Smith records. She also taught me to guzzle moonshine that she bought off a big hammerheaded guy named Hambone. Hambone got a thing for me. This he demonstrated by hanging out at Molly's one night, giving us free moonshine. After a few hours, we were all catatonic. When Hambone walked, he made gushing sounds, the liquid swirling through his enormous dugonglike gut. Clyde had passed out and Molly had carried him into the bedroom, where, I suppose, she was taking advantage of him. Hambone, still fairly alert, was focusing his nefarious attentions on me.

"So why ya do that?" he drawled at me.

"Do what?"

"That shit to your hair. Whatcha got blue hair for?"

"I like it."

"Un. Yeah, well, I guess I could get used to it." With this he narrowed his reptilian eyes to slits, leered at the crotch of my purple pants, and wondered, I suppose, if I tinted my pubic hair as well. "Why doncha lie down on your back on the floor there." He waved his paw at the rug.

"What?"

"I don't mean nothin' nasty. I'm sayin' lie down, I'll pour some 'shine down ya throat, it's good that way."

"Oh. Okay." I obliged. He poured the wicked liquid into my gaping maw. As the moonshine burned down my throat and sparred with my stomach lining, Hambone applied his lips to mine. I waited a moment, gauging whether this was simply repugnant or if was perhaps sexy as well. At which point Molly suddenly appeared: "Zoe, Hambone, what the fuck?" she wailed. Hambone jumped up with an alacrity I never guessed he possessed.

"Uh, sorry, Molly, I got, uh . . ."

"You get your ass outta here now, 'Bone. GODDAMN!" Molly stamped her foot the way you would at a bad dog. Hambone hung his big head and wordlessly made tracks out to his pickup truck.

"Zoe!" Molly reprimanded. I shrugged and looked sheepish. "That's gross, Zoe, I mean, I understand you get drunk and any pair of pants looks good, but come on, he's not even a pair of pants, he's a TREE, Zoe. And he's a married tree. Got five rugrats, too."

I kept away from trees after that and evolved up the food chain of married Southerners. I fell in love with Nicholas the Horse Thief.

One day, I was lurking around the stable, performing menial tasks in exchange for being allowed to ride one of the Thompsons' fox-hunting horses. I was pitchforking slabs of soiled straw into a wheelbarrow. I won't say I was the embodiment of adolescent sex appeal. I was skinny with a big horse-riding ass. My hair, blue with brown roots, hung in limp strands. And I was wearing enormous khaki pants, a hand-me-down from Charlie, who wouldn't let me wear black around the barn. A voice said, "So you're the filthy little punk rocker, huh?" I spun around, brandishing the pitchfork.

"Hey, easy, girl," the guy said, throwing his hands up in surrender. I lowered my weapon. He let out a low whistle, the sort that came out of Charlie when considering a particularly good horse. "Why, you're beautiful," the guy said. "I'm Nicholas."

"Oh," I said. That explained everything. This, then, was Nicholas the Horse Thief. Nicholas extended his hand, very formally. I put my paw in his. He raised it to his lips and planted one on my fingers. He was easy on the eyes, in a craggy, horse thief sort of way. He

LOOKED like a horse thief. Charles Bronson goes cowboy. Of course, he wasn't exactly a THIEF. He was just a little unprincipled. Sold people's expensive horses on consignment, then neglected to pay them. Either they came at him with a lawsuit or a gun or he went out of town long enough for them to forget. Or he simply charmed them. I'd been hearing about Nicholas's stunts for so long, he was practically part of my personal mythology. Lately, according to Charlie, Nicholas had been trying to go straight. He was on to his third wife, this one a very upstanding sort of girl who was reportedly changing Nicholas's ways. But it only took one look at him to know that this was an impossibility. I don't know if Nicholas had decided before ever laying eyes on me that he was going to seduce me, his old friend's underage daughter, but, in retrospect, I think I always figured I'd have more than a passing interest in him.

"I didn't mean nothin' by that remark, Zoe. You didn't take it wrong, did you? Just that your old dad's been kinda worked up over how you look. I been hearing about your hairdos ever since you started living with him."

"Yeah. Well. It's okay, I guess. " I ran a hand through my hair and felt awkward.

"The whole town's talking about you."

"Oh yeah, well, I've heard a little talk about you, too," I said.

He laughed at that. "Yeah, you're Charlie's daughter all right."

He was having an effect on me.

"I'm gonna take you to lunch tomorrow. Nicest place in town," he announced.

"Oh?"

"Sure. Twelve-thirty. You'll be ready?"

"I guess, yeah."

"You guess? What, darlin', you got a previous engagement?"

"Yes. I mean no. Twelve-thirty."

"I'll see you then," he said. He kissed my hand again and then walked away. He had a beautiful ass.

The lunch was at an old-fashioned Southern place. We said very little. Afterward, he kissed me lightly on the lips. This was enough to provoke a haunted two weeks of pining until I saw him next. Which was at the big party following the foxhunt. Molly, as caretaker of the hunt's horses, had finagled me a horse so that I, too, could go fox-hunting. Foxhunting struck me as bizarre but interesting. People dressed in tight pants, red coats, and black velvet hats. Got on a horse. Got a bunch of hound dogs and other similarly attired people on horseback. Ran like hell, following the hounds, which were ostensibly chasing a fox over many miles of countryside.

I put on my outfit, mounted my horse, a big sweet chunker named Meatball, and hung on for the ride. I had a flask of whiskey which I imbibed in too much and, an hour into the hunt, fell off of Meatball. Molly caught him when I came tumbling off. She brushed me off, admonished me for my budding alcoholism, and, once I was safely back in the saddle, led us on a shortcut to catch up with the rest of the hunt.

That night was the hunt dance at Mr. Thompson's mansion. I wore my lone dress, a morbid loose black frock found in a thrift store. Charlie and I walked in and Charlie, spotting a girl he was interested in, went off to follow that bliss. I got eyeballed too much and skulked off to a corner, finding refuge in a plush ottoman next to a sweet old octogenarian who turned to me and introduced herself: "Hello, dear, let me say that that's a *lovely* dress. These kids today just don't know how to look presentable. My name is Sally Eldin."

"Hello," I said, taking her proffered paw and shaking it.

She engaged me in conversation about peach cobbler and the works of Faulkner. Two things she was fond of. We were ensconced in a line-for-line analysis of the first paragraph of *As I Lay Dying* when Hambone appeared and wedged his large ass down between Mrs. Eldin and me.

"Hello, ladies, hope I'm not interruptin' nuthin', but y'all's the belles of the ball and I had to get me an eyeful." Oh good, more mock-ery, this time from someone who had in fact applied his sizable maw to mine. Mrs. Eldin, too old to take the compliments of fat rednecks at anything but face value, said, "Thank you, young man, you're looking dashing yourself." This a stretch of even her generous octogenarian's aesthetics. Then, as Hambone's fetid breath heated my neck, I saw Nicholas at the other end of the room. About a dozen people were gathered around him, hanging on every word of whatever tale he was telling. His wife was on his arm. She was pale and blond and looked very tired.

A little later, as Hambone fed Mrs. Eldin shots of moonshine from a flask at his hip, I skulked away to find a bathroom. I walked in, and before I'd latched the door shut, Nicholas materialized and slipped into the bathroom with me.

"Hello, darlin'," he said, closing the door behind him.

"Uh . . . Hi," I said.

"I'm sorry I'm married and I'm sorry you're fifteen," he said then, flapping his large blue eyes at me. Well. That about summarized it. Nicholas put his lips to mine and the ornate trappings of the bathroom turned to fat clouds through which Nicholas and I flitted, spinning, twirling, and spewing endearments and vows of eternal bliss. His hard hips ground against me and I wanted, more than anything, to be inside *him*, to sit and lurk in a remote recess of his spleen or heart or liver, to be a cell inhabiting his physical being. Then there was a knock at the bathroom door and fear lashed Nicholas's face like a vicious whip. "Just a minute," he called out. He looked around the bathroom, seeing, I suppose, whether there was a hamper he could stuff me in. There was not and eventually he had to open the door. Fortunately, it was just Mrs. Eldin. "Howdy, Sally," Nicholas said, turning on his electric smile.

"Well, hello there, Nicholas," said Mrs. Eldin.

"I was just helping Zoe here, she was feeling a mite under the weather," Nicholas said.

"Oh!" said Mrs. Eldin. "There you are, dear girl, Hambone and I wondered what became of you. You will come back to sit with us, won't you?"

"Oh, uh . . . I'm not feeling that good, I dunno, Mrs. Eldin."

"Well, dear, I understand." She patted my hand, then went into the bathroom. Nicholas winked at me and went off in search of his wife.

A few months passed, then Charlie was offered a job in Pennsylvania. Having uprooted me too much as it was, Charlie, who didn't know what was going on between his daughter and his best friend, asked Nicholas if I could live with him and his family while I finished off the school year. Nicholas generously agreed. And so I went to shack up with Nicholas and his wife and kids. Which turned out to be less ideal then I'd envisioned. For one thing, I was miles away from Molly and Clyde and now had no one to hang around with. Nicholas was often on the road, horse-thieving in other states, and so I kept company with Nicholas's young sons, Blackie, who was four, and Remy, who was eight. We would hunt snakes and capture bugs until Nicholas's wife, Wendy, inevitably came looking for us, thinking no doubt that I was corrupting her kids as well as her husband. Wendy never said a word about what was going on with me and Nicholas. She must have known, though. We still hadn't consummated our heat but we snuck kisses and feels at every turn. It was hard to miss.

I also hung around with a farmhand named Link. Link was a formidable man with blueish black skin and a slow smile. He showed me how to grow flowers and vegetables in a small garden behind his trailer. These we fertilized with an ample supply of manure that I often helped him muck out of the horse's stalls. At night I'd sneak out to his trailer and we'd smoke joints and drink wine. Once, he kissed me, a gentle soft kiss. I responded. He stopped then, shook his head, and said, "Yup, just what I need, get caught with the boss's teenage piece o' ass." He shooed me out of his trailer then and we only saw each other in the daylight.

Eventually, school was over and it was time to go up to Charlie's new digs in Pennsylvania. Nicholas, to my horror, was away.

Ironically, I'd ended up seeing less of him when I was living in his house than I had previously. Now I was leaving and our tenuous love was going to go unconsummated.

I had packed up all my things, gone on a final snake hunt with the kids, and, once she was asleep, pilfered weed from Wendy's stash and gotten very high. I lay on the couch bed, spinning my emotional wheels.

"Zoe," came a soft whisper. I sat up. It was dark in the living room but I could see Nicholas's form as he came to sit at the edge of my makeshift bed. "You were gonna leave without giving me a kiss?" Nicholas said. He put his hand on my foot.

"You're here?"

"I think so, darlin'."

"I thought you were in Florida."

"I was." He squeezed my foot, then reached under the sheet and found my hand.

"Come on, get up." He pulled me to my feet. I was wearing only a long battered Sid Vicious shirt. I followed Nicholas outside. Moonlight was falling in long slabs over the exterior world. The farm, by night, looked lush and spooky. Nicholas wrapped his arm around me and we walked out toward the field beyond the barn. I was barefoot and the dirt felt good and real beneath my soles.

We stood for a while in the middle of the field. Nature was sending up soft sighs, releasing what was trapped inside of me. The trees breathed, the world breathed, I did not. Nicholas and I pressed against each other and kissed, soft slow kisses unlike our usual quick fevered gropes. His hand shook as it went under my T-shirt and traced shapes on my skin. Then I froze. I no longer felt the lust of our grope sessions. I was afraid of heart wounds. I was just plain afraid. Nicholas was taking off his clothes, at first slowly, then very quickly. Suddenly everything sped up, like a vicious puck was standing nearby with his pudgy finger on the fast-forward button. Nicholas was naked and he was now lying stiffly on top of me. I was a fifteen-year-old floorboard beneath him. I couldln't see his face. His eyes, the shape of his mouth, were all obscured. There was simply a weight on top of me, and his dick, probing between my thighs. Maybe, once we were actually fucking, the sensations would course through me and burst. They did not. Nicholas's breath came faster, then he exhaled tiny bullet sighs and collapsed by my side.

"Put your shirt on, darlin'," he said then. I sat up and blinked at him. He was getting dressed. He wasn't looking at me. I was waiting for something. And it never came.

We walked back to the house. I thought of a lot of things to say but did not say them. He pecked me on the cheek, then went into his and Wendy's bedroom. The next morning, as I stood on the porch, bags at my side, waiting for Molly and Clyde to take me to the airport, Nicholas came out, put his hand against my cheek, and said, "I'll see you again, Zoe. And I'll keep you here." He pointed at his heart.

I shrugged. Yeah, right. I felt hard and mean.

Molly and Clyde had agreed to drive me to the airport and now pulled up. We loaded my stuff in the trunk and drove off, smoking joints and listening to Patti Smith.

9

Burning Holes in the Hearts of Many

I really am an idiot to *still* be sitting in Satan's closet. It is quite late by now. Later than I know since my watch stopped. It is the watch given to me by Edgar, who was the boyfriend before Oliver before Bev before Satan. It is a beautiful antique watch but it doesn't work very well.

I don't know what's keeping Satan, and I'm getting bored with my vigil. To amuse myself, I've started foraging through the drawers of the furniture *thing* I am sitting on. There are photos. Arty photos of European shopfronts and things. And here, Satan's infamous photo of a monkey jerking off in the zoo. Satan loves to tell the story about the monkey jerking off. It took its small red monkey dick into its fist and beat its meat till it spurted into its own eye. This story somehow stirs Satan.

In his honor perhaps I will now masturbate in his closet. Why not. I will masturbate in Satan's closet while thinking of Bev. This is, coincidentally, the first time I have felt like masturbating in weeks. Which means one of two things. Either Satan's closet is the biggest turn-on in existence or the poison must be out of my system. You see, my humble hovel, which I have perhaps presented as sweet if slightly disheveled environs, is in fact poisoned. This realization came to me the day they carted Billie May away to Bellevue.

Billie May was one of the quietest people living in the building. If you passed her in the hall, she'd shiver up against the wall, apparently afraid that contact with another human might contaminate her.

Billie May probably ended up in Bellevue because of the building poison.

The reason I know the building is poisoned is that I have had a month-long headache and have lacked, as I mentioned, the energy to fuck myself. Obviously, something is wrong.

My friend David the Sex Addict, who attends our Idiots Anonymous dinners but is also a member of the more formal Sexaholics Anonymous, fucks himself raw and also fucks anything that moves and some things that don't. He has fucked Coke machines and sheep. Men, women, dogs. You name it, he's fucked it. He's a really nice guy. He just can't stop fucking. He has lost jobs and housing and lovers because he can't stop fucking.

Now David goes to Sexaholics Anonymous, where, he says, they say masturbation is a slip. Fucking yourself equals falling off the sex wagon.

I, thankfully, am not a member of Sexaholics Anonymous. Masturbation is not a slip for me. Which is a good thing because I have a theory: Masturbation leads to productive behavior. The release of orgasm makes me want to get up and vacuum.

The reason I think I must always have productive behavior is probably my mother Francine's fault. Francine is now a martyred saint of the work ethic. She works twelve hours a day while still maintaining a brutally clean home and a huge stock of tuna noodle casserole in the freezer. From dawn till dusk, my mother performs backbreaking labor at a horse stable, then rushes home, dons a cute checkered apron, and bakes her face off so that she and her third husband, Marty, can eat well. She stocks approximately fifty-two dishes of casserole in the freezer so that when my brothers and sister and I come to visit, there will be food for us. My mother, Francine, is a wizard, a lithe and muscular goddess of the work ethic, a compact amazon with steely blue eyes and short no-nonsense hair. You wouldn't want to fuck with my mother. She might impale you on a pitchfork and feed you to the horses. Although, of course, horses are vegans.

But I do love my mother, even if she has made me rub myself repeatedly raw. At this point in our lives, we are basically complete strangers, but there is love there. Which is why my friend Jane is endlessly nagging me to invite my mother for a weekend on Sixth Street. Jane thinks that I should invite Francine to New York, show her the sights, and go see *CATS*.

The thought of *CATS* has probably almost never crossed my mother's mind. The thought of spending a weekend in my shitty little hovel with me probably scares my mother even more than it scares me. Probably, we would both die if this happened. We would not know what to say to each other. We would be two awkward strangers standing in a shitty hovel getting ready to go see *CATS*.

"So, Mom, you ready to go see *CATS*?"

"Yes, Zoe, I'm ready to go see *CATS*."

"Okay, Mom, then let's go see *CATS*." And off we'd go, two strangers going to see *CATS*.

As it happens, I already saw *CATS*. This is almost unbelievable. If you could see me right now, you would know I am not a *CATS* type of girl. I am sitting in my ex-boyfriend's closet with my hand down my pants and a chain in my lap. I am smoking a filterless cigarette. I have a sort of psycho existentialist look going. Under my pants, I am wearing boxer shorts. My slightly stubby fingers are inside the fly of the shorts.

Although I was wearing boxer shorts the day I heard them carting Billie May away, I did not wear boxer shorts on the day I went to see *CATS*. I wore something that was an attempt at looking as much like everybody else as possible. I think it was a knee-length black skirt and a white shirt. All the same, I didn't look quite like everybody else. No matter how I dress, people who don't know me invariably say: You must be in the arts.

I went to see *CATS* with my grandfather and my two half brothers, Julian and James. Neither Julian nor James nor I would dare tell our grandfather that the idea of watching half-assed actors dressed up like pussycats in public—the idea of witnessing such a thing was not something we dared tell our grandfather we were not into. We want him to like us. When he wants us to go watch prancing pussycats on Broadway, we go, we totally go.

Except my sister, Louise. My half sister, Louise, didn't go to see *CATS*.

Louise works in a dog food store. She is nineteen. She goes to college part-time and works in a dog food store. She calls me only sporadically. Most recently, I had a message from her on my answering machine. It went like this:

"Zoe, thith ith Louith," she lisped. "I juth got my tongue piethed and I'm all numb. Call me. Bye."

Louise wears men's boxer shorts. For a minute, she thought she was a lesbian. My half sister, Louise, very much *wanted* to be a lesbian. From ages fourteen to sixteen Louise had sex with a boy who was her boyfriend. From seventeen to nineteen she did not have sex. At nineteen she had sex with her best friend, Samantha. They had been friends for years. Samantha was and is a lesbian, and, to Louise's way of thinking, the Coolest Girl in the world. One night, Samantha seduced my sister, Louise, and Louise liked it. They were just lying around on Samantha's bed. Samantha's mother was at the office. She is a gynecologist. She instilled in Samantha an acute awareness of her own body. Samantha is very comfortable with this body. She wrapped it all over Louise's body. This was before Louise had her tongue pierced. She only had her ears pierced. Samantha had her nipples pierced. Louise fondled Samantha's nipple rings and then Samantha went down on Louise. They had fun. Louise said, "Girl sex is great." She told me the day after it happened. Called me and said, "Girl sex is great. I think maybe you should try it."

"But, Louise, I have, I've tried it, but I like men better. I mean, I don't really know what to do with tits, you know?"

"Oh, well, I do," Louise said. She said it like I was inferior. I was a Sexual Neanderthal for wanting to fuck men. I am. I'm a Masturbating Idiot and a Sexual Neanderthal. Welcome to my life. Watch out for the poison.

So then, after Samantha fucked my sister, she didn't call her. I was really angry. I wanted to go kick that little bitch's ass. Finally, my sister had had a meaningful sexual experience, and the person responsible for it was being an asshole. I wanted for this kind of thing not to happen to my sister. Because she is years younger than me, I feel like her mother. Maybe she in turn feels like she's supposed to invite me to see *CATS*. But, of course, she lives in Delaware. *CATS*, as far as I know, is not playing in Delaware. Besides, Louise probably feels more like she needs to take our mother, Francine, to *CATS* than me. I am just her sister.

I wanted to kick that little dyke bitch Samantha's ass.

All the same, if someone brought a bunch of girls dressed in men's underwear over to my house, although it wouldn't be my ultimate sexual fantasy, it would be fun. It would pull me out of this post-love slump and bring back my predatory side, the side that emerged when the first man I loved was cruel to me. When I turned to spreading the misery around. When I rose up, a vicious fanged predator, burning holes in the hearts of many.

And so now, if someone brought me a bunch of women dressed in men's underwear, and I could do anything I wanted with them, maybe, just to see how it felt, I would say, "Okay, you bitches, down on all fours and lick my floor." Then I would giggle. And if they *did* happen to get down on all fours and lick my floor, I would have to tell them to stop. I would feel too bad for them to take pleasure in their discomfort. It would be different if they were boys. A few years ago, after I'd fallen for and then been emotionally trounced by a beautiful but demented boy named Rick, I traveled to Morocco with my friend Elizabeth the Former Speed Freak. In Morocco, I very much wanted twelve naked boys to do my bidding. To maybe even get down on all fours and lick my floor. I wanted them to lick my floor and dance naked and writhe around my cheap hotel room.

When Elizabeth and I set foot in the Port of Tangier, dozens of

Moroccan boys swarmed around us offering drugs, hotels, and miscellaneous gadgets. While Elizabeth was overwhelemed by the rush of brown hands and eyes and the smooth pouty lips that promised everything, I was excited. Slightly afraid but excited. All the same, for safety's sake, I didn't announce that yes, I wanted twelve naked Moroccan boys writhing in my hotel room. Because we were two white chicks loose in Morocco, I kept it to myself.

Although we were on vacation and productivity was not required, I did in fact masturbate frequently in my tiny green hotel room. From my window I could look over the buzz and hum of the ancient marketplace. I would stand there naked, just out of view, spying the sea of faces, the fluid movements of young boys, the veiled women, and the men, harsh, shouting, barking, and laughing through the bulging streets. There was a sleepy eroticism in it and I pranced around my room naked, no boxer shorts, nothing. I straddled my pillow and rubbed against it rhythmically.

Elizabeth was usually out shopping while I rubbed myself raw. She was an unemployed drummer. The only time she made money off drumming was when she and I were both in the girl band SLANG. But Elizabeth didn't need to make money off drumming. She was an heiress. As such, she did a lot of shopping there in Morocco. Each morning, she would shop while I masturbated and made vague attempts at writing down potential fuck book scenarios. By midafternoon, she would come back, toting bags of baubles.

"Look what I found," she'd say, unfurling sacks of beads, perfumes, and leather goods.

She'd languorously fondle her loot, her graceful fingers lingering on each item. For Elizabeth, shopping in Morocco was as much of a turn-on as the sleek pouty-lipped boys were for me.

One day, Elizabeth bought a pair of skintight brown leather pants that she tried on for me, asking if I thought her boyfriend, a toothless guy named Westy who fixed Harleys for a living, would appreciate the exact nature of her curves beneath the taut skin of dead animals.

"Oh, he's gonna love that look," I said, motioning to the place where the leather molded her crotch. I could, unfortunately, well imagine toothless Westy *gumming* Elizabeth's leatherbound pudendum, which was rather a revulsive image.

The way I saw it, Elizabeth should be swimming in a sea of sexual and intellectual demigods. Yet, for reasons I could never entirely piece together, she honed in on scabby downtrodden sorts who were not only physically unkempt but were psychic and financial leeches as well. Elizabeth had some sort of heinous guilt complex about her wealth. Accordingly, she associated with scabby boys and impoverished chicks like me. It was by her graces that I was there in Morocco. She had "loaned" me the money. This she had done without hesitation, but whenever Tensions of Travel thrust forward their fat necks, the "loan" became a palpable tightness between us. Mostly, the Tensions of Travel were, as I saw it, the annoying cloyings of her heart: She spent several hours a day composing long letters to Westy. How she had time to experience the things she was writing him about, I don't know. When she wasn't shopping or writing, she was out in search of fax machines that were few and far between in this crook of Tangier. Sometimes, when I groaned at the prospect of another afternoon in search of a fax machine, Elizabeth's lips would draw tightly together. A thick vein in her forehead would begin to visibly throb a warning: I paid for you, don't complain. And I tried not to. I was, after all, more than anything, jealous. Although I didn't want to fuck Elizabeth, I certainly had a crush on her and wanted her undivided attention.

After a week, Elizabeth had bought up most of Tangier and I had tired of this particular city as masturbatory fodder. We decided to rent a car and drive to the city of Fez, which, depending on who you asked, was either two or sixteen hours away. No one in Tangier ever agreed on anything. Least of all how far away Fez was.

The car rental guy warned us about our travels: The easist road to Fez was the Kif Road. The road used to ship truckloads of that green demi-weed from one city to the next. The Kif Road, Car Guy said, was lorded over by Kif Bandits. Crazed kif smokers who would lie down in the middle of the road playing dead, then, as soon as you got out of the car to check on the prone body, would spring to life, bonk you on the head, get in your car, and drive away, cackling diabolically and firing up a *spliff.*

These warnings nonwithstanding, we embarked upon the Kif Road. Morocco unfurled for us her ponderous bag of charms, fields of nubile green turning to desert, mounds of sand skimming an ocean of impossibly blue sky. Here and there, slow-moving dots of brightness: Berber peasants in multicolored robes leading donkeys over the dunes. No Kif Bandits, though.

Elizabeth drove with concentration, every so often pulling off to gawk at the savage beauty of things.

"You could never capture this kind of beauty, could you?" she said, putting down her Leica and motioning at burnt hills from which sprang angry fistlike shrubs.

"Uh, no, I guess not. . . . Hey, can we eat soon?" I said, raining on her aesthetic parade. Not that I was immune to beauty, just that dwelling on it somehow diminished the immediacy of it.

Elizabeth said nothing to my food request but did stop at the next roadside café, where, peasants had hitched their donkeys to a sort of banister that ran along the outside of the café. There were also cars, and from them poured upwardly mobile Moroccans in need of a mid-travel snack. We walked in and the collected eyeballs of fifteen or so men rolled up and down us like greasy marbles. Elizabeth went to the counter to order tea. I went hunting for the toilet, which turned out to be a sort of seething meat locker. A tiny shard of light came in through a fissure at the top of the wall. Layers of slime and decaying waste painted the walls dark green, and an ammonia stench penetrated, then raped the nostrils like a dozen frenzied monkey dicks in intercourse. I pulled down my pants and peed into a hole that gawped out of the floor's center, like the inverted black eye of a perverted Cyclops that was going to jump up my crotch and feed on my innards. I made it out of Lucifer's toilet in one piece and found Elizabeth seated at a little table, busily composing yet another love letter to Westy. I repressed a growl and sucked down my tea. Eventually, we shoved off, back down the Kif Road, slowly progressing toward the elusive Fez, which was proving to be a lot more than two hours away. Finally, by evening, we arrived.

Fez was less Westernized than Tangier, and within moments of our checking into a slightly ominous hotel, it seemed the whole town knew of the arrival of Two White Chicks. Once we'd put our bags in the room and washed our faces, we went out to look for food and found half a dozen boys camped out there, wanting to be our guides. We picked a little fat boy whose name, he said, was Raoul to guide us into the heart of the town, the *medina*, whose ancient twisted streets were labyrinthian.

Of course, first Elizabeth had to find a fax machine. Raoul said that he could not get us to a fax just now. There was one in a sort of breakfast restaurant that only opened mornings. Tomorrow we could go there. Elizabeth made a moue of disappointment but then recovered, and, in her inimitable fashion, began to engage Fat Raoul in a conversation about his shoes. Elizabeth could engage anyone in a conversation about anything. Where as I was introverted, surly and picky about who I would talk to, Elizabeth was a happy puppy, pawing at and charming humans the world over. After exploring for a while with Raoul, Elizabeth and I gave him a few dirhams, then settled in at a little café where we ate hard-boiled eggs and sipped mint tea.

"God, it's so magical here," Elizabeth said, gazing off at the elaborate mosaic tiling on a nearby doorway.

"Yeah, it sure is," I said, eyeing a young Moroccan boy sitting two tables away.

Elizabeth was less than thrilled when I struck up a conversation with the Moroccan boy. I had crossed over some sort of boundary. I was asking for trouble.

The boy's name, he told me in awkward English, was Abdoul. He was lithe and had enormous black eyes. With him was a friend, also named Abdoul. Abdoul 2. Both Abdoul 1 and 2 were wearing Elvis T-shirts. This Elizabeth liked. She complimented the Abdouls on their

Elvis T-shirts but was all the same annoyed with me when I asked the Abdouls to walk us back to our hotel. She was convinced that by flirting with them, I was asking for *it*. We had reread Paul Bowles before coming to Morocco and now, as we walked to the outskirts of the *medina* with the Abdouls, Elizabeth thought these nice boys were going to suddenly summon a tribe of gnarled sub-dwarf cohorts, bonk us on the head, tie us up, drag us to some dank basement, and fuck us till our eyes popped out.

We stopped off to look at some ancient tombs buried in the dry hills that surrounded the city. Elizabeth stood nervously talking with Abdoul 2, while Abdoul 1 and I darted off behind some stubby trees. There was a low-hanging moon. Abdoul and I stood face-to-face, then inched closer. I pressed my lips to his. At first, the peril of kissing a nineteen-year-old Arab in the middle of Morocco was profoundly enticing. I felt like William Burroughs, Paul Bowles, or any number of brilliant white perverts who had come here to churn out books and fuck half the population. But then, as Abdoul's lizardlike tongue darted into my mouth, I found it tasted distinctly of *dead gym socks*.

I pulled away. Abdoul 1's black brows shot up in questioning arcs, then, attributing my reticence to some sort of White Chick Mood Swing, he shrugged. We walked back to where Elizabeth stood near Abdoul 2, wearing a pinched expression and barely containing the lecture she had in store for me.

Back in the safety of our hotel room, as Elizabeth furiously dug out her writing pad and pen, preparing, I supposed, to relate my bad behavior to Toothless Westy, I announced that I had kissed Abdoul 1.

"You didn't," she said.

"Yeah, I did. Why not?"

"Because, Zoe, we're in Morocco. Kissing is probably tantamount to marriage. They're probably baking you some sort of twenty-tiered Moroccan wedding cake as we speak. I mean, what were you thinking? You can't possibly be serious. Tell me you didn't do that."

"Okay. I didn't do that."

"Good," she said.

But I had done that. And the next morning, the Abdouls were waiting for us outside the hotel. I don't know what they had done with Raoul, who had been scheduled to come take us to the fax machine. Maybe paid him off in punches and sent him packing. When Elizabeth asked after Raoul, the Abdouls made vague gestures. "He was going to show me where the fax machine is," Elizabeth said.

"Ah, we have fax machine. We will go there," Abdoul 1 said authoritatively. Elizabeth brightened at this. The Abdouls told us about the day they had planned for us. They would take us first to the leather factory, which, they said, was something we didn't want to miss. Then on to the fax machine, and later we would go to Abdoul 1's sister's house for a *tagine* dinner. Elizabeth and I wanted to get some breakfast but the Abdouls protested: No, we had to be completely empty-bellied when we arrived at Abdoul 1's sister's. It would be rude to not eat everything that was put before us. The Abdouls ordered us to fast. They were vehement about this, and I caught Elizabeth's face clouding over as she shot me a look: *See,* said her two blue eyes, *they are baking a wedding cake and they are going to tie us up and fuck us till our eyes pop out.*

I shrugged at her and we followed the Abdouls to the leather factory, which we had imagined as some quaint place where Moroccan leather bags were fashioned. A stench hit us as we ascended narrow stairs into an enormous courtyard. Greeting us was a fly-swarmed pile of cattle extremities. It looked like a thousand little Lucifers had stopped in this spot, divested themselves of cumbersome hooves and horns, then gone on to tend to Important Lucifer Business.

Near this pile sweltered another one made of innards that oozed, congealed, and baked there beneath the sun. Elizabeth and I gaped at this and the Abdouls laughed. "Ah, does it disgust you?" said my Abdoul, his beady eyes ignited by his attempt to shock me.

"Oh no, I love it, really." I said, watching his face register disappointment. Abdoul 1 had not and perhaps never would evolve beyond pinching and poking as demonstrations of affection. My attempts to discourage this just added fuel to his fire, and he pulled and pinched that much harder. He tugged my hair hard as we watched the remains of some poor cow get dyed blue.

When we had fully toured the stinky factory, we moved on, presumably toward the fax machine. An hour later Elizabeth and I had sufficiently recovered from the leather factory experience to realize we were starved, but when we tried to buy some figs off a vendor, both Abdouls flipped their lids and screamed Arabic somethings at the fig vendor, who then would not sell us any figs. This small scene caused a crowd to gather and stare at the white chicks being screamed at by two Abdouls and a fig vendor. Elizabeth and I tried to melt into the ground and resigned ourselves to the Abdoul-imposed fast as we glumly trudged farther into the *medina*. Abdoul 2 chattered to Elizabeth about Crosby, Stills and Nash, of whom he was inexplicably fond, and Abdoul 1 continued pinching my skin to a bruised pulp.

As we walked, veiled women stared at us and giggled at our weird clothes and skin color. Dark-eyed men whispered things and smiled. The Abdouls began to sing Crosby, Still and Nash songs in unison as Elizabeth and I grew increasingly uneasy. Hours went by like this, walking, stopping here and there to look at a beautiful mosque or a rug store. When, late in the afternoon, we finally reached the purported location of the fax machine, we found the storefront boarded up. The Abdouls scratched their heads and shrugged. Elizabeth blanched. Panic came into her eyes. I don't know what she thought would happen if she didn't get her missive off to Westy. Perhaps that he would, upon not hearing from her for a day, go off and gum some other girl. I don't know. It took her a half hour to recover from all this. She insistently quizzed Abdoul 2 as to where there might be another fax but he didn't know. Finally, she resigned herself to the horror of it all and gave up.

It was evening now and we were walking deeper and deeper into the maze of tiny streets. Any second now I supposed, we would come face-to-face with the Minotaur who would help the Abdouls tie us up, fuck us, kill us, and cook us. Elizabeth had been right: I was wrong to flirt with the Abdouls. A horrible fate awaited us.

It was after nine P.M. when we got to Abdoul's sister's. She lived in the Moroccan equivalent of projects. A tenement building of four stories where something like sixty families lived. There were no walls. Blankets and plants hung to indicate where one abode started and another stopped.

The entire population of the building stared in wonder as we traipsed up some fragile stairs, walked through twelve different families' homes, and finally arrived in Abdoul's sister's place.

She was a thick, dark woman who glared at us malevolently. She apparently had had no idea that Abdoul was bringing us. She spoke only Arabic and she now said a few mean-sounding words. Abdoul 1 said some mean-sounding words back. He then said, "This is my sister Cherifa. She welcomes you to her home."

Now my heart did a panicked jig. For one thing, Cherifa was *definitely not* welcoming us, and for another, her name was *Cherifa*, the name of Jane Bowles's Moroccan lover, who had, by some accounts, *poisoned* Jane Bowles and ultimately *killed her.* This was our Minotaur. And she was formidable. She had seventeen chins, cafeteria lady arms, and the breath of a dead dragon. Elizabeth gave me another "I told you so" look, and by now I knew she was right. We were *fucked.*

Abdoul and Cherifa spat vowels at each other a while longer. Ultimately, Abdoul 2 stomped his foot and hissed out something that I loosely translated "If you're not nice to the white chicks, I am going to pull your head off your neck stem." Cherifa finally narrowed her eyes, spat on the floor, then snatched up a large basket and stormed out of the place. When she had gone, Abdoul 2 told us that Cherifa was off to buy food so that she could cook for us. Elizabeth said this really wasn't necessary , we didn't want to put Cherifa out, and would the Abdouls mind showing us the way back to the hotel now.

This flipped them out.

"We have brought you all the way here for my sister's hospitality and now you want to LEAVE?" My Abdoul was beside himself. He glowered at me. His face ballooned and went purple and his eyes popped out like some Elvis-worshiping Arab comic book character. "Oh no, we're just kidding," I protested weakly. "We wouldn't dream of leaving."

Abdoul was mollified. His eyes went back in their sockets. Elizabeth and I plunked down on a threadbare rug and tried to behave ourselves.

By the time Cherifa stormed back in, her basket swollen with produce and a headless chicken, another hour had passed and our appetites had grown fangs. Elizabeth and I volunteered to help peel vegetables, but Cherifa threw filthy looks at us. We went back to our rug and watched the Abdouls get seriously snockered on illicit wine that they had bullied off of a neighbor. As they drank, they began to sing along to the Rai music that was screeching out of a decrepit cassette player. Rai music is Algerian pop music and sounds something like Nine Inch Nails with Arabic vocalizing. It wasn't very pleasant, particularly with both Abdouls singing along, for the Abdouls, among their many attributes, were without question tone deaf.

Cherifa, adding perhaps to the feast's cooking time by inbuing all the food with White Girl Poison, was taking forever. Elizabeth and I cowered and starved and waited. Time stood still. Then Abdoul 1, who was by now really shitfaced, sat down next to me and commenced to pinch, poke, and pull all at once. I was no longer amused. Nor did I give a shit if he or his sinister Minotaur sister liked me. Although I was totally at their mercy in the middle of Morocco, a girl can only take so much. I snarled. I grabbed his hand, bent it backward, and, putting my face an inch from his, said, "STOP IT." Abdoul howled something murderous in Arabic and grabbed hold of my own hand. Cherifa turned, multiple chins quivering, chicken neck in hand, and glowered, Abdoul 2 glowered. Elizabeth glowered. Abdoul then crushed my poor paw in his and raised his other hand as if to hit me.

I squeezed shut my eyes and said, "NOOOOO." Then, suddenly, Abdoul laughed. I slowly opened my eyes. He dropped my hand and kept laughing. Then Abdoul 2 laughed, then Cherifa laughed. Finally, even Elizabeth started to laugh. The joke was lost on me.

When Abdoul had stopped cackling, he faced me and said, "You are not for me. I love someone else. You cannot have me."

Ah, I thought. Bummer, dude. Abdoul then said something to Cherifa. Possibly "Don't feed her, she is no longer my betrothed." Or "Feed her amply, imbue her food with poison, choke her, kill her." Cherifa shrugged and began scooping food onto serving plates.

His love for me dissipated, Abdoul was instantly more cheerful. He said happy-sounding things in Arabic. He motioned for us to all sit down around the platters of food. Even Cherifa seemed more amiable as we gathered on the floor, forming a circle around the feast. The food was a maw-melting blend of flavors and consistencies. A just reward for the tortures of the evening. But before we had finished feeding, we felt our welcome getting worn out. Now that I was no longer Abdoul 1's intended, and since Abdoul 2 had already made Elizabeth swear to send him dozens of Crosby, Stills and Nash cassettes, they had no use for us. We'd barely gotten one hot sip of mint tea before the Abdouls sprang to their feet and acted fidgety.

Elizabeth and I stood up. Cherifa, by now virtually beaming, bid us farewell and the Abdouls escorted us out of the building and into the *medina*. They took us back to the hotel by a shortcut, and the walk that had taken something like nine hours on the way there took a mere twenty minutes back. Which was good, since there seemed nothing more to say. They walked us to the hotel driveway, then immediately turned back toward the *medina*, hightailing it away, their voices gaining in volume as they went, already comparing notes on the absurdities of white chicks. Elizabeth was too exhausted to throw any "I told you so"s at me.

We returned to Tangier the next day. Elizabeth went fax machine hunting like a thousand-dollar-a-day dope fiend looks for his fix. My appetite for writhing Moroccan boys had been curbed. I no longer had the slightest desire to burn holes in the hearts of young black-eyed things with limbs that flow like a naughty river. I didn't even masturbate. I realized that my powers to burn holes in the hearts of many were strictly Western Hemisphere powers. Accordingly, I waited till I was back in New York to do any burning.

My half sister, Louise, got burned by Samantha. Samantha fucked my sister, then never called her again. That little troll burned a hole in my sister's heart. Louise, as a result, moped around for several months. I would call her up: "Hi, Louise, how's it going?"

"Oh, I dunno."

"What's the matter?"

"Nothing."

"Come on, tell me."

"Well, I dunno."

"Who should I ask?"

"Tthh. Hhn." This disturbing sound was the closest thing to laughter I could pull out of her.

"Well, what? What are you doing? Are you having more girl sex?"

"No."

"Why not?"

"Well, what am I supposed to do? Go up to girls and go, 'Hi, I dunno if you're gay or not, but would you like to see my boxer shorts?' "

"But don't you have radar or something? I mean, can't you *tell* if girls are gay or at least bi or not?"

"No," she said, "I can't. I mean, this one girl came in the dog food store and she was really cute and she was wearing these baggy pants and like had these boxer shorts hanging out of her pants and I sort of took this as a sign, so then I was explaining how much crude protein her dog should have every day—she had this beautiful German shepherd—and I told her about the protein and then I asked for her phone number and she like totally freaked out and left the store and the next time I saw her she was with this big fat guy and she had her arm around him and she just looked *totally* hetero."

"Oh," I said then. And then I dropped the subject. And then, a few weeks later, Louise in fact met a boy and fell in love with him and now she is convinced she is hetero. Even though she wanted to be a lesbian. For the moment she is not.

Francine would probably have a heart attack. We don't know for sure, but both Louise and I figure our mother, Francine, the Goddess of Horseshit and Tuna Noodle Casseroles, doesn't want queer kids. Part of why Louise *wanted* to be a lesbian was to shock Francine into acknowledging her. Surely lesbianism would get her attention. More than *CATS* would.

When we went to see *CATS,* my brothers James and Julian and I sat there wedged in the theater seats next to our grandfather, who already had a CD of the soundtrack to *CATS* and was therefore familiar with all the *CATS* songs. Our incredibly proper Republican grandfather sat humming along to *CATS* as James and Julian and I twitched in our seats and pinched and elbowed one another, trying to repress guffaws and chortles as the half-assed actors dressed like pussycats leapt around in tight outfits and sang songs.

Julian and James and I don't see one another more than twice a year now, but when we do, we usually mention the *CATS* episode.

"Remember when we saw *CATS?* And they had on those *outfits?* And Grandfather was *singing* along? And you guys kept *pinching* me and I almost *died?*" And then we laugh and guffaw and chortle for forty-five minutes.

Louise refused to see *CATS.* Our grandfather even bought her a ticket, but when Jim and Julian got on the train to come to the city and see *CATS,* Louise did not. She was fifteen then and she wouldn't do anything. Now my grandfather is not paying part of Louise's college education. Because she dropped out of high school and went to work in a dog food store and only recently got a high-school diploma and started going to college. Because of this, she has to pay for it.

When my best friend, Jane, first said, "Let's invite Francine to come up and see *CATS*," I don't think she understood how funny that was. Even though she meant it as a joke, she only meant the *CATS* part as a joke. To me, the idea of inviting my mother to spend a weekend with me was a much bigger joke than *CATS*.

Of course, since I have actually seen *CATS*, I won't sit through it again. But maybe I *will* invite Francine to visit. Maybe I will burden Francine with my insecurities, for which she was, after all, the blueprint. Maybe a Mike Leigh play will be off Broadway. Maybe Jane and I will take Francine to see a Mike Leigh play. She might be shocked at the frankness of it. She might not. She might surprise me. Maybe I could go so far as to turn to her in the theater and say, "Mom, I've been meaning to tell you, I fuck myself *stupid* every day for several hours in an attempt to be more *productive*," and she wouldn't bat an eye.

Maybe she would not be shocked at all. She could be full of surprises, I don't know. I don't know her but perhaps I will try to.

Billie May had the sort of face on which shock no longer registers. Too much had happened in her face for shock to live there, too. The few times I ran into Billie May, she was standing in the hall uncertainly, fidgeting with something on her person. She had a lot of attachments. Weird key chains and pieces of clothing hung off of her. She was probably fifty or so years old. She was probably the same age as my mother.

It was probably just the flea spray that was poisoning me and making me unproductive. It was probably the flea spray that got under Billie May's skin. The whole building has fleas and has had fleas for some time now. This happened when Daisy the Stripper fell in love with the No Ass Squatter from the gutted building next door. The squatters have dozens of dogs with fleas. Their fleas got on Daisy's dog and now have spread to our whole building. My cat is scratching himself raw. The exterminator is beside himself. The exterminator, when he comes, knocks on the door and says "Exterminator" in a really weird way. It is straight out of David Cronenberg's movie interpretation of William Burroughs's *Naked Lunch*. The exterminator looks like Peter Weller playing the William Burroughs character in *Naked Lunch*. Once, I tried to explain this to the exterminator. He just looked at me evenly and said, "You're in the arts, aren't you."

Billie May went totally ballistic. She shot Mikey the Heavy Metal Guitarist, who lives in apartment 4C. She shot him in the leg. No one knew little old gray-faced Billie May had a gun. Least of all Mikey the Heavy Metal Guitarist, who lived directly above her. Had he known, he might have thought twice before playing that Led Zeppelin lick over and over and over.

Billie May pounded on his door. Six flights down, I could hear her pounding and screaming, "You fucking CRETIN. You masturbating idiot."

Masturbating idiot? I thought, What, was she spying on *me*? But then I realized that, for one thing, I am not masturbating much, and for another, "masturbating idiot" is just how Billie May thinks of second-rate rock guitarists. I did not hear the shot. Maybe it was muffled by pieces of her clothing that got in the way. I don't know. Next thing I knew, there was screaming and people racing up and down the stairs, and eventually the ambulance came and carted the Heavy Metal Guitarist off to the hospital. He was fine. The bullet only grazed his tibia. Billie May is probably not fine. They took her away. She is gone. She is in a locked ward. She is another casualty. Another heart burned full of holes. The kind of holes that cannot be filled.

How much the flea spray had to do with it, I don't know.

How much the flea spray had to do with my lack of masturbatory fervor, I also don't know.

Now some alternative rockers will probably move into Billie May's vacant apartment. Maybe they will feel the ghost of Billie May. Probably not. They will pay five times as much rent as Billie May was paying. They won't like Mikey the Heavy Metal Guitarist either.

They will be a generation younger than him. To them, Led Zeppelin is good only for kitsch value, not as something you actually learn to play.

To them, maybe Nine Inch Nails is something you learn how to play over and over and over.

And now I've got my paw stuck deep down in my boxer shorts. But I can't really seem to get comfortable. Maybe I will come out of the closet and go hump one of Satan's pristinely clean pillows. Although I would come off pretty deranged if Satan came home just as I was climaxing on his pillow. I guess that no matter how you slice this twisted pie I am going to come off pretty deranged. This is a deranged situation.

10

Idiot Unleashed

After Georgia, I joined Charlie in western Pennsylvania. We lived in a suburban housing complex a few miles from the farm where Charlie was working. I was no longer as much of a freak as I had been in Georgia. Weird hair and dark clothes, although not de rigueur adolescent garb, were more accepted here. I still felt mean and hard and this, I suppose, gave me an edge. I spent my time hanging around with the neighborhood burn-outs: Seth the Walking Acne Scar, Jilly the Slut, and Cameron the Geek, who'd dropped acid one too many times. We'd sit in a little clearing in nearby woods, doing bong hits and listening to ACDC or, at my insistence, an occasional Clash tape. One day, the burn-outs were going to get some speed from John the Garbageman. He was older, nineteen. He had a car and a job and the others spoke of him with reverence.

We walked over to the other end of the housing complex to meet him. He was wearing dark clothes and leaning against a black car. He looked like a sort of emaciated speed freak James Dean. Which is to say, I found him devastatingly attractive. He basically ignored me as Cameron the Geek negotiated the transaction and Jilly the Slut stood by quivering to get his attention. But later on, after I'd popped two Black Beauties, then gone home to listen to Patti Smith and draw furious little sketches of my room, the doorbell rang. Charlie was not around. Actually, Charlie had gotten married. This almost a side note since she, the wife, a French Canadian named Bette, simply appeared one day. He'd met her sometime when I was still in Georgia, had mentioned her in passing when we spoke on the phone, and had, by the time I came to join him in Pennsylvania, married her. They did not appear to like each other much, but, for once, they were actually out doing some sort of couple thing.

And so I was alone, mildly bonkered on Black Beauties, when the doorbell rang. I opened up and there stood John the Garbageman. He was smoking a filterless Camel and looked slightly nervous.

"Hope it's okay, Cameron told me where you live. You wanna go for a ride or something?" He ran one hand through his greasy black hair. His lip twitched involuntarily, shot through with a speed spasm.

"Oh . . . uh . . . yeah . . . uh . . . lemme just, uh . . . okay."

We didn't go very far. Got in his black Dart, drove to a remote corner of the parking lot, and sat there smoking nervously. He gave me some coke to snort. We kissed. We almost bit off each other's tongue in the process. We liked each other. For the next month, we went out every night. Most of the time this involved parking somewhere near my house, snorting bad coke, smoking pot, not talking much, and making out. Sometimes I accompanied him on Minor

New Bliss was a quaint sort of town. Its economy was b⌐
tourists and gay guys. Accordingly, the parents of kids at school
shopkeepers, basket weavers, B&B owners, and the like. Hippies. A⌐
their kids were burn-outs. The whole school was burn-outs. I was
comfortable there. Still socially inept, though. It took a few weeks to
really make a friend, but when I did, I really did. We met smoking in
the bathroom. I'd noticed her in math class. Always came in late.
Passed out with her head on her desk. Sweet-talked her way through
things. Her name was Hope and no one fucked with her. That much
you knew from one look at her. She was tall, chesty, and blond but
played down her looks. I was awed by her when we first met. We were
standing near the bathroom sink.

"You got a cigarette?" she said, looking through me.

I lit one and gave it to her. This an intimate gesture that served to
get her attention.

"Thanks," she said. She inspected herself in the mirror, was
pleased with what she found there. She eyeballed me.

"Like your pants," she said, pointing, with her chin, at my baggy
purple pants.

"Thanks. I like your shoes." They were black and sleek.

"Thanks. Capezios. My uncle's a dancer. He's gay. Of course."

"Of course."

"You're new."

"Yeah."

"You got any pot?"

"Yeah."

"Good, let's go."

We went out back by the football field and smoked. We both liked
the Clash and speed and decreed that high-school boys were pimply
bores and what we really needed were real men. Pierced and dyed
punks who, at that time, were still a scarcity in these regions.

Hope and I were instantly inseparable, developing an entire
lifestyle and language together in the space of a few weeks. We wore
each other's clothes and slept at each other's house. She would visit

my little cabin, I would hole up with her in the room she shared with her little brother and sister. Her two older sisters had both started having kids at age fourteen and were by now firmly ensconced in hideous apartment complex studios, leading sad Welfare Mother Lives. Her own mother, Fran, was a hot tomato with codependency problems. She had an antiques shop but opened it infrequently. She was too involved in the sordid demise of one or another ill-fated affair. This also kept her away from home most of the time and so Hope and I basically had the run of the place.

We soon developed a fondness for crystal meth before math class. Whereas we had previously both been complete math imbeciles, now we began to have some real skill with numbers when our brains were buzzing like a hundred angry bees making foul algebraic honey. Our taste for meth became such that we had to actually go get jobs to support our habit.

We got hired on at the Holiday Inn while some sort of maid strike was happening. We were scab maids on speed and we were coming to clean your room. A crotchety old bitty, Mrs. Jensen, the maid in charge, assigned us our maid uniforms. Hope's was too tight and the skirt barely covered her ass. My own was big at the neck and hung down so that my nipples constantly threatened to pop out.

For our first day of work we hoovered a small mound of meth that lit a fire under our cute little teenage asses as we pushed our maid cart into the first room. We plowed through the place, excising each and every speck of filth. By the fourth room, however, our attention waned. Now we didn't feel like ruining our gloriously amphetamized heads with cleaning. We turned on the vacuum so it sounded like we were vacuuming, used wads of moist toilet paper to pick pubic hairs out of the tub and off the sheets, then sat down and, using the convenient Holiday Inn stationery and pencils from the bedside table, began to play game after game of Hangman.

By our second weekend working there, we had it down to a few economical strokes of the duster and, of course, the disgusting but necessary picking out of pubes. Then one Sunday, at nine A.M., after a rough night of speeding and playing Scrabble, we came face-to-face with the scummiest room in the history of filth. We had heard from our boss that some junkie record producers were holing up in there. They had now gone antiquing for the morning, leaving their sty for us delouse.

There was slime and blood in the sink; dense hairballs, remnants of some sort of fevered pube-removal session, choked the drain. Dead socks, cigarette butts, cheeseburger carcasses, and crusty underwear decorated each surface like sick Christmas ornaments. It was so filthy we actually had to clean. This infuriated Hope, and to exact her revenge on these slovenly sub-dwarfs, she began searching their belongings. Pretty soon, she hit the jackpot. A fat Baggie of Quaaludes. We did not think anyone would have the nerve to call up the front desk and say, "The maids stole my 'ludes, man." And so we pocketed these horse pill–sized delights, did as much cleaning as we could bear, then moved on.

Our shift was over at noon, and before we'd finished the last room, we each popped a Quaalude. We hitchhiked from the highway, where the Holiday Inn sat like a gestating prefab condor, back into town. We did not change out of our maid outfits but went instead straight to a diner for a late breakfeast. Just as we prepared to order enormous feasts of egg and sausage and pancakes and grits, the 'ludes hit and our limbs turned to rubber. As a pretty-boy waiter tried to make sense of us, I felt myself falling into a deep pool. Hope managed to place our order, and as the waiter walked away, Hope said, "Check out his ass."

"Yeah, it's okay, but isn't he gay?"

"Oh no, he's bi," Hope assured me. She was, as ever, right. By the time we had finished wrestling with our breakfeasts, she had, on rubbery legs, swaggered over to the waiter and whispered something in his ear.

Somehow, an hour later, we three were up in his room, which was conveniently located above the diner. I immediately collapsed in a corner and, my blurred eyesight bringing me triplicates of both Hope and the waiter, watched in wonder as she expertly pushed him back onto the bed and began to yank at his zipper.

I felt like an embarrassed idiot as I watched Hope pull her pink maid tights down with one hand while hoisting the skirt over her ass with the other. The waiter began signaling to me to come get in on the fun. Not wanting to come off as a prude, I made an attempt at wobbling over. I got within inches of their gruesome intercrural lock, then collapsed on the floor. Hope was now riding him. I don't know how she was managing such coordination. She was like a gymnast on Quaaludes. I closed my eyes. I swam in a warm pool of numbness. I began fantasizing about various members of the Clash, my fingers playing through their stubby haircuts, my tongue tasting their green-paste complexions and nubby, thin British limbs. This worked so well that I could feel a tongue down my throat, pink, pale, possibly pierced. I opened my eyes and this was no Joe Strummer tongue, it was Hope's tongue and it was swapping fluids with my own. The waiter took this as a cue to hump my thigh. I tried to stand again. The waiter fell over onto his stomach and started humping the floor. Hope, suddenly realizing that she and I, by swapping fluids, had now crossed some boundary that we as hetero teenage chicks did not really care to cross (this was, after all, 1980—a decade before teenage bisexuality became a requirement of alternative culture), now turned away from me and threw herself on the waiter. I passed out.

I came to many hours later. On the floor. Hope and the waiter were strewn across the bed. Just as I began to test my legs, Hope woke up. She methodically put her clothes back on, looked at me evenly, and said, "Let's go see about copping some speed."

There was never any mention between us of this incident. We never saw the bisexual waiter again, and we were fired from the Holiday Inn, where, presumably, the slovenly record producers *had* complained that the maids stole their 'ludes.

Time traveled quickly now that I had a cohort. We were always up to something. Shoplifting, speeding, smoking, holding down various awful jobs from which we were always fired. And then Charlie, in one fell swoop, divorced Bett, told off his boss of the moment, and announced that we were moving to New York State. For once, I made a scene. I refused to leave Hope. Hope refused to let me leave. With a surprising minimum of fuss, Hope's mother, Fran, agreed to let her come with me and Charlie to New York. One afternoon, Fran came over, bringing with her some papers a lawyer had drawn up wherein she relinquished seventeen-year-old Hope to Charlie's care. And so Hope came with us.

We lived in an apartment over the barn in New Rochelle, New York, a very posh Westchester suburb. By now, Hope and I had cut off all our hair and dyed it orange. We wore either all black or sickening color combos. Lots of dog chains around our necks. No one at New Rochelle High School would talk to us except a handful of Deadheads who we basically hated but had to make nice to in order to buy pot. By now I was smoking about a half ounce a day. This disgusted Hope. I was dopey and dull. She tried to find us a speed connection but had little luck. We started popping Dexatrim and other foul over-the-counter fake speed. We had halfhearted love affairs. Mine was with Joe, a military fatigue–wearing Deadhead who worshiped Iggy Pop and was therefore ostracized by other Deadheads. Joe and I had sex only once and neither of us was entirely sure that we *had* had sex since we'd been in a mutual blackout from thirteen hours of drinking shots of Jack Daniel's. But we liked each other as best we could. We saw in each other holes that needed filling.

Hope had a fling with a guitar player named Jeff, an emaciated straight A student whose hobby was to learn every song Richard Hell had ever written or played on. Jeff was much shorter than Hope and liked to be smothered by her impressive breasts. This I know because I watched. Not particularly as a turn-on, but just because wherever Hope went, I went.

Sometime in the middle of eleventh grade, a guidance counselor paid Hope and me a visit. He was a tiny, nervous man named Mr.

Wine, who swallowed our story that Charlie was away for a month, and announced to us that we were flunking out. He tentatively proposed regimes of night school but seemed relieved when we both said we would just resign from high school.

We tried to keep this from Charlie for as long as possible. Charlie, by now, was involved with a borderline-psychotic eighteen-year-old with a coke problem and a pair of psychiatrist parents who had had her on medication since age two. She kept Charlie busy but eventually he did notice that Hope and I weren't going to school. He then put us to work. Hope as a receptionist for the stable, me as a groom, mucking horseshit, and brushing horses, saddling them up for the snotty rich girls who came to take lessons. I developed impressive biceps and a bad attitude. Manual labor was not suited to my temperament. I was, by now, a poet. I composed vicious verse for the one-chord punk songs I wrote on my imitation Les Paul guitar. I started to slack off at work and spent hours and hours holed up in Hope and my room, smoking bucketfuls of pot, playing my one-chord songs, and talking to my pet sparrow, who I had nursed back to life after finding him half squished in a horse's stall. I was losing whatever tenuous grasp on reality I'd possessed.

Charlie fired me. I was ostensibly supposed to go out and find another job but instead stayed in my room. Then a few things happened. First Charlie's psychotic girlfriend became convinced that Charlie and Hope were having an affair. This we found out about when I was suddenly awakened one night, as Hope and I slept, each in our twin beds. It was dark in the room but I could sense something creepy. I didn't move but tried to focus my eyes. I saw a glint of silver and, honing in on its source, saw Lynnie, Charlie's girlfriend, standing over Hope's prone form, holding a knife the size of Kansas. I was frozen. My heart thuttled and thwomped in my chest. Finally, just when I'd started forming a vague plan of attacking and de-knifing Psycho Lynnie, a low animalistic moan, a sort of wild-goat-in-heat sound, began emanating from her. The goat moan lowered in pitch and began to come in short bursts, snatches of what I deduced was laughter. Lynnie was a happy psycho about to do away with my only true friend on the surface of this floating earth. Then, in the next millisecond, before I was about to spring on her, Lynnie turned the knife on herself, aiming it at her heart. She continued to laugh, very softly. Then she simply turned around and walked out of the room.

The next morning, in her inimitably casual style, Hope said, "Did you see Lynnie trying to kill me in the middle of the night?"

I'd had no idea Hope had been awake and aware of her near demise. I hadn't even been planning to tell her about it because I wasn't fully convinced it *had* happened in real life.

"Yeah," I said. "I saw her."

"I think I'm gonna go back to Pennsylvania," Hope said then.

I was horrified. I pleaded and begged, but this is how Hope was. She made a decision in a split second and then stuck to it. She was tired of our life in New Rochelle. I was a hopeless pothead and did nothing but sleep and play guitar badly. She was now supporting my pot habit with her receptionist wages and I wasn't even good company. Never mind the fact that Hope would probably be bathed in her own blood before the week was out. The next day, she packed up and left.

About a week later, as I slinked further down into the crevices of my personal hell, fortune intervened. I was playing guitar, very loudly, with the windows open. I kept noticing a disturbing knocking sound in the distance. I finally put it together that someone was knocking at the apartment door and went to see who it was. A sort of aging sex kitten, her hips made all the more voluptuous by her tight riding britches, stood there on the door step, smiling at me. "So you're the rock star?" she said as I opened the door and blinked furiously, my eyes shocked by sunlight.

"What?" Who was this vixen and why was she mocking me?

"I hear you playing guitar every time I come here," she said. This she said not as an accusation of noise pollution but simply as a fact.

The vixen, it unfolded, was manageress of a glitzy Manhattan recording studio. To whip her decaying curves into shape, she had taken up riding. She was sort of an anomaly at the stable, which catered mostly to nubile rich girls. Her name was Rosie, and for some reason she decided to take me under her wing. She brought me into Manhattan one day to look at the recording studio where she worked. I walked around marveling at the place. It was a vast and padded womb into which no daylight shone and through whose passages walked guitar-toting guys with funny hairdos and coke-addled engineers whose skin had never seen sun. In a word: heaven. Rosie and I walked in and out of various studios where sessions were going on. She showed me the plush lounges where record producers holed up making phone calls and orchestrating various acts of world domination. She then brought me into her office and sat me down behind an enormous beautiful desk.

"How does that feel?" Rosie said then as I sat engulfed by the desk and grinning stupidly.

"Feel?"

"You like sitting there?"

"Oh, well, sure, yeah."

"Good. Come back Monday morning. You're hired." And this, then, was my big break as a recording studio receptionist. I was still only seventeen and Charlie had to sign papers permitting me to work, which he did without hesitation.

Within a few months, I'd put away enough money to get my first hovel, a tiny studio apartment on Ludlow Street, on the Lower East Side. I bid adieu to Charlie. We weren't on very good terms now. This perhaps because he was, from the depths of drunken debacles with Psycho Lynnie, losing his own grip on reality and saw in me his personal insanity refracted and spat out in a hundred little orange-haired punk rock shards.

By day I worked in the womb, answering phone calls and flirting with minor rock stars. At night I holed up in my hovel. Ludlow Street was at that time a teeming leper colony of downtrodden Puerto Rican families, junkies, and a few oddball white kids like me. A block away was thriving heroin territory, a mini-empire of slum bums and enterprising black and Puerto Rican boys with sawed-off shotguns, pitbulls, and a maniacal grasp on the capitalism of addiction. From my window I watched junkies in lines that extended an entire block. They shuffled, coughed and spat, waited their turn to dash into the guts of an abandoned building, emerging moments later with their dope secured in their underwear or shoes. The cops busted the place once a day but this only put a minor damper on things. It was a thriving little empire.

My lone friend was a gay guy named Jody who lived next door. Jody was a flamboyant beauty. Much prettier than me. He worked at an art gallery and had an infallible sense of style. He molded me into a punk vixen and sometimes we went clubbing together, but invariably he would find some unsuspecting straight boy whose dick he absolutely had to try to suck. He would abandon me in the bowels of the club and go off to chase pipe-dream dick. Sometimes I would dance around by myself. Occasionally, I'd go home with a boy. These encounters were tenuous, awkward, completely unmemorable save for one French boy who, after a less than dazzling one-nighter, decided he loved me. He would appear at my door bearing roses, bonbons, and cat food for the various strays I took in. He was so eager, it scared me. I'd let him in, then ignore him. After a few weeks, he gave up. Then I missed him but had long thrown out his phone number.

Gay Jody had a taste for heroin. Soon I did, too. It was more economical than weed or downers. One little sniff and a thousand bricks came flying in the face of my uncomfortable consciousness. It was a pleasant existence. But I missed Hope. I called her in Pennsylvania, where she was busy acquiring a flat Pennsylvania accent—this a mystery since she had never, in seventeen years of growing up there, had one, but now mashed vowels as if they were Twinkies to be flattened and spread on the palate. Without too much prodding, Hope agreed to abandon her job taking care of retarded people and come live with me in the hovel.

She brought with her a bag of clothes and a little black-and-white

TV that one of her retarded clients bequeathed her when she left the 'Tard Farm, as she fondly called the place.

"So this is it?" she said witheringly as I welcomed her into the tiny studio we would now share.

"Yeah." I shrugged defensively. It wasn't much but it had to be better than Pennsylvania.

"Well, Zoe, we've got to get some furniture. I can't be living like a savage."

"Okay, that's fine. We can do that," I said, placatingly. The next day, Hope dragged me to various furniture stores, where she greedily ogled plush couches and vivid rugs. These, of course, were far beyond our means. And this infuriated Hope. "I'm gonna have nice stuff," she said, setting her mouth into a determined thin line, then storming away from these furnishings-beyond-her-means.

A few days later, although she did not succeed in filling our hovel with Sotheby's remnants, she did land both a waitressing job and a sugar daddy named Rene. He was a medical student from the Upper East Side and a mysterious figure to me because Hope would never introduce us. I suspect she thought that if Rene laid eyes on me, an unrelenting specimen of post-punk uncoothness, he would start to see that Hope was not the innocent but chesty thing he thought she was. She had, for all I knew, told him she was a virgin.

Pretty soon, Hope's latent domestic gene grew and thrived. She became a Happy Punk Homemaker. She was a brilliant Dumpster diver and would come home toting the glorious refuse of society. From an the Upper East Side Dumpster she rescued an exquisite Art Deco dresser. Near Columbia, a slightly tattered but perfectly beautiful Moroccan rug. Our hovel was getting a warm glow.

Hope could cook, too. Mostly Steak-Umm sandwiches, Steak-Umms being a hideous thinly sliced meat product that we found unspeakably delicious. Or grilled-cheese sandwiches. Nothing terribly high-tech but all of it more than I would have done on my own.

Hope and Gay Jody got on famously and soon the three of us had little dope-sniffing parties. None of us had a habit yet and so it was all in good fun. Jody would score. We'd all three sniff, then either nod out or, if we were ambitious enough, go clubbing. Hope and Jody, in fact, got on so well that one day they actually fucked. This was apalling to me, since I'd always harbored a crush on him and she, within a few weeks of moving in with me, had scored. One night, I came home from work and found Hope standing in the bathtub, which was in the middle of the room. It was an odd time to be bathing and Hope looked terribly sheepish. "What are you doing?" I asked.

"Nothing. Bathing."

"I know that. But you never bathe at night."

"What, I have to answer to you when I want to take a bath?"

"No, God, I'm sorry, I was just curious."

"Pfffh," said Hope. A few minutes later there was a knock at our door. When I opened up, Jody was standing there, holding up a pair of Hope's panties, "Darrrling," he drawled, wiggling the panties at the end of his pincers, "Hope left her panties near my bed. Advise her to please be more careful. I mean, reeeallly, what if I had a date? How would I explain *panties*? Ga!" he exclaimed, handing over the offending item.

"Cha cha cha," he trilled with a little wave, then turned and walked back to his own apartment. I couldn't figure out why he and Hope had bonked in the first place. And Hope was certainly not forthcoming about it. Hope was, in fact, rather circumspect about sex. Although we had had our little "orgies" in the past, and this should have served to make us forthright on the subject, such was not the case. She finished bathing, put clothes on, and said, "Shall I fry us up some Steak-Umms?"

Jody would not teach us, as we wanted him to, how to cop dope for ourselves on the street. Probably because by copping for us, he could tap our bags, hogging that much more for himself. But we didn't mind any of this. We didn't really have habits yet. This came a few months later, and as soon as it did, we worried. We gleaned from studying the pages of *Junkie* that the flu symptoms we began to exhibit were in fact withdrawal. And so Hope called down to Pennsylvania and had some crystal meth sent up so we could speed our way through this unpleasantness.

The meth came the same day as Fred the Cat, a large tabby who appeared at the window and demanded to be let in. I opened the window and gave the sweet beast a bowl of milk. He lapped this up, then nestled on my bed, I monikered him Fred and decided to keep him.

A little later, after Hope and I had hoovered huge quantities of meth, I gave Fred the combing of his life. His once-dull fur now sparkled and barked with color. Fred preened as Hope and I embarked on an all-night series of Hangman and Scrabble games. Our heads felt like they had sprouted little crystaline wings; they flew and fluttered and hovered like amphetamine angels, looking down into our neck holes and the sacks of flesh and bone that were our bodies.

When eight A.M. rolled around, we did a few booster lines to get us off to work. My job at the womb was hard to bear that day. I was far above the floating earth, circling with increasing velocity. But at least I did not feel the awful dope withdrawal symptoms.

By the third day of our Speed Regime neither Hope nor I could go to work. Our mouths would not form words. Our bodies would not perform the dull series of movements required to get us out of the apartment. It was on this day, as we sat losing the ability to even concentrate on the Scrabble board, that we noticed the bugs.

Hope saw it first. We'd both been scratching a lot. And now Hope noticed little white bugs diabolically navigating the surface of her skin. She pointed an accusing finger at poor Fred. "That cat gave us FLEAS," she exploded.

"No!" I protested, scratching all the while.

"Yes! He goes or I go," Hope said haughtily. She banished poor Fred back to the fire escape from whence he came. He sat for a moment outside the window that Hope had slammed shut. Fred looked at me mournfully, then, doing a cat's version of a shrug, went away: Have it your way, humanoid freaks.

The next day, after still no sleep but a lot of scratching, Hope, in a sudden fever of domesticity, went to do the laundry. She came back sans our clothes but bearing a large paper sack.

"I got bombs," she said, pulling canisters from her bag. "We're gonna kill those fuckers," she snarled, brandishing a bomb like a heartless Fumigation Goddess.

"Where's our clothes?" I asked tentatively.

"Huh?" she said, wheeling around and looking at me with enormous, accusing pupils, as if I were an overgrown flea.

"You took our clothes to the laundromat, right?"

"Oh, SHIT," she said, hitting herself in the forehead and dropping the flea bombs. She raced back out, returning about an hour later, foaming at the mouth and carting our bag of clothes, which she had apparently left in the flea bomb store and never taken to the laundromat.

We threw the bag of laundry in the closet, then set off the bombs and went out to wander the streets while this systematic flea decimation took place. We walked around, scratching ourselves and chewing the insides of our lips. The sun seemed to burn holes in us. The exterior world looked like a particularly overpopulated and seething tier of inferno. People looked like so many tiny insects, their faces unformed, their heads sprouting globiferous antennae.

But it didn't seem to work. We came back to the hovel, snorted a few more lines, then, as we got ready to settle down and count specks of dust on the floorboards, we saw them. The bugs were still with us. In fact, they appeared to have multiplied in the flea bombs' wake. They were perhaps an example of organisms that restructure their own DNA to survive Adverse Bug Conditions. They were self-manipulated parasites and they were angry as fuck. They bit us ferociously, they swarmed in great white clouds around our heads, attacking our every orifice and mound. Hope screamed, "FUCK, they're gonna eat our *faces* off." She raced to the window, opened it, and started hurling all our stuff out onto the fire escape—clothes, towels, chairs, even our beds. She piled our entire lives out there on the fire escape.

We set off four more flea bombs and vacated the premises. This time, we headed right out of the city. Went to Grand Central, where we caught a train to New Rochelle. We were going to descend upon my unsuspecting father. As we sat on the train, fidgeting and trying not to scratch too obviously, we began noticing that our bugs were getting tired of us as hosts and were paying their respects to the business commuters. We saw some poor lawyer swat at his head with annoyance, dropping a Bible-thick stack of subpoenas in the process.

"We better move to another car," Hope hissed in my ear. "They're gonna figure out we've brought the bugs. Come on."

As we barreled into the next car, all eyes turned to us. It seemed as if all the commuters were in psychic communication: *Look out, lady,* the lawyer had mentally intoned to the little gray bitty who now regarded us with hairy eyeballs, *two speed freak punk chicks with a pesticide-resistant strain of parasite upon their person traveling your way. Lady, run, don't walk, to the other end of the car.*

By the end of the train ride, we had infested every car. We cowered out of the train station and arrived at my father's apartment with our flea-bitten tails between our legs. Charlie, thankfully, wasn't too surprised at our sudden visit, nor did he see any reason to question our desire to hole up there for a few days. His girlfriend was out on a day pass from a psych ward and so he had his hands full.

Hope and I settled into the living room and tried to watch *The Love Boat* to take our minds off the infestaton. Our theory was that the fresh air of Westchester County would kill off our parasites. We knew we should probably be sitting outside, in this fresh air, to facilitate the bug holocaust, but the light hurt our eyes and so we stayed in the living room. Then, to our horror, we noticed Dingo, Charlie's sweet and devoted German shepherd, scratching with a vengeance. Now we had infested the poor dog. This was too much. We left Charlie a note and headed back to the train station.

"We're gonna have to go to the emergency room," Hope said now as we settled into the thankfully mostly empty train.

I agreed that yes, we were going to have to go fess up to some member of the medical profession: It was us who had infested an entire commuter train of citizens and my father's poor dog, too.

We hit Manhattan, then raced into the Bellevue emergency room. By now our skin was raw from scratching. "You do it," Hope said. "No point in us both seeing the doctor since we have the same bugs. You see the doctor and get the medication, then we split it."

"Oh, come on, you do it, please?" I begged of her. Doctors terrified us both. But since Hope did all the domestic stuff, I apparently was now relegated to the task of making an imbecile of myself for the doctor. "Pardon me, Doctor, but I have fleas. And not mere fleas these, good doctor, no, crafty little devils who've manipulated their own DNA, recombining it, gently coaxing it to resist any pesticide humans may have crafted. Help me, Doctor, my skin sack is in your hands."

Hope at least agreed to walk with me up to the front desk and describe our plight to the nurse. There was a long line of sorrowful souls. Old ladies dragging one leg, mothers fattened on Welfare Cheese Product, carrying dirty-faced kids. As we waited for the nurse, a guy walked in missing a chunk of scalp. Really, the back of his head was just *gone*. He stood there for a few moments, bleeding less than you would think and blinking furiously. Eventually a doctor noticed him and gently coaxed him behind a curtain, where presumably they filled in his head wound.

When at last our turn came, I looked at the nurse and said simply, "We have bugs."

"I beg your pardon?" said the nurse,

"Some sort of fleas," I said in a low voice.

"I'm sorry, I couldn't hear you. What?"

"I said we've got FLEAS, LOOK!" I let loose, proffering my raked arms.

The nurse backed away a few inches. Then, dryly: "Do you live near a garbage dump?"

"Of course not," Hope intervened, "we had a cat. It had fleas. Now, please get us a dermatologist, we're *highly* contagious."

The word *contagious* lubricated the wheels. The nurse sprang into action and soon I was whisked away to another floor, where, in record time, I was tended to by a doctor. He had a huge ginger-colored beard and little spectacles rested at the end of his long nose.

"Please, take a seat," he said in faux-amiable doctorspeak. "My name is Dr. Hansen. Now, what seems to be the trouble?"

I launched into the tale. The cat. The fleas. The fleas breeding and multiplying, the contagion. He examined me, prodding, dabbing, and puzzling at length.

"Tell me," he said at last, "have you been taking any hallucinogenics, miss? LSD? Mushrooms?"

"Certainly not!" I said, sticking my chin in the air. Ha. Acid? Me? No way!

"Are you *sure*?"

"Yes I'm sure, I don't do *that* stuff."

"Well, have you been sleeping? Eating?"

"Of course! Well. Okay, not *that* much. I've been having trouble sleeping."

"And you haven't eaten in a while either, isn't that right?" he said, motioning to my stick-figure limbs, which indeed had not been fed in nearly a week.

"Well . . ." I conceded.

"You're having hallucinations. There are no bugs of any sort. Yes, you have scratched yourself and made scabs," he said, gesturing at my poor arms, "but the marks on your arms are only from scratching. I suggest you eat and then get a good night's sleep."

I was mortified. Then I tried to hit him up for a sleeping pill script, but the good doctor was, I'm afraid, on to my act and shook his head gravely. "No, you'll sleep on your own. It is unwise to become dependent on medications at a young age. Now, if you'll excuse me . . ." And he was gone.

I went back to the ER and found Hope, sitting in a corner, fidgeting and scratching. "Stop scratching," I hissed at her, stinging from the humiliation of the ginger-bearded doctor. Hope, who hadn't seen me coming, jolted a good foot off her seat. "Huh?"

"It's all in our heads, we don't have bugs."

"Impossible!" said Hope, motioning to the cloud of bugs around her head. I could still see it, too. But I was willing to give the hallucination theory the benefit of the doubt.

"Come on, we've got to eat," I said.

"Eat?" Hope sneered.

And eat we did. Well, choke on tiny pieces of toast that we ordered at the first diner we found. We were each successful in holding down one slice. And, sure enough, a few minutes later, the itch began to go away. The white cloud dispersed. As we rode the bus back downtown to Ludlow Street, we still had residual itching but it was lessening. When, the next day, we woke up after a deep twelve hours' sleep, the bugs were all gone.

Somehow, though, the bugs got to Hope. She was not the same after that. Another month or so passed and then, once more, she went back to Pennsylvania.

11

Demeaning the Devil

I still have my hand down my pants as I go through more of Satan's drawers. I need more evidence of what an asshole he is. Then, bingo, a box of syringes. I don't know if this means he's back on dope or if maybe he now has to *shoot* his assorted antidepressants, anti-panics, and anti–FEEL ANYTHING.

When I first met Satan, he was coming out of a paranoid coke stupor. He told me this about a week into our liaison when I stepped on a crack pipe stem in his bathroom. As he extracted glass fragments from my foot, he told me that just a week before we'd met he had been holed up snorting, smoking, shooting coke, and watching the NBA play-offs on TV. Sometimes a bath of heroin to bring him down. This binge was brought on when his feisty girlfriend of five years, a girl he referred to simply as Joe, had packed up, moved out, and immediately shacked up with some hip-hop producer with pants that put his ass crack on display. But now our "love," and I use the term loosely and in quotes, "saved" Satan from the medicinal grips of his coke and dope mistresses. Yes, he took to boning me and drugs became a thing of the past. But Satan never jumped through hoops for it the way that I did, Satan never performed menial tasks for dope. Maybe he should have. Maybe I will make him. I will chain him and make him. I'll run out and buy a gun. I'll come back. At gunpoint, I will force him to perform menial tasks. Of course, I won't give him drugs as a reward. No. There will be no reward at all. He will perform menial tasks for free. Yes. But first maybe I'll go get Jane. Jane and I will giggle as we stand there, holding Satan at gunpoint and making him clean out the toilet with his tongue.

Jane and I will reenact the scene of our first meeting. When Arthur the Drug Dealer was forcing *me* into menial labor. Yes, we will demean the devil and laugh. And laugh. And laugh.

12

He Throbbed,
She Quivered

Arthur was a drug dealer who thought of himself as an artist. He had, once upon a time, painted. By the time I met him, he didn't paint anymore, dealt dope and coke to hipsters. He maintained a sort of salon there in his loft. He was Gertrude Stein on the pipe, and, to this end, gave free drugs to people who had made films or records or paintings. Classic dealer stuff, really: gave it to them a few times, then once they'd acquired a taste for it, made them pay.

Arthur seldom left his lair, and with each passing month increasingly resembled an overgrown vegetable. His skin became an impossible orangish gray, his eyes seemed to burrow deeper into enormous sockets. Some combination of coke, dope, and malevolence was causing his face to retain water, giving his head the look of a melon forever on the verge of popping open and spraying juice all over the music and film equipment that various dope-addled hipsters had hocked to him for a gram here, a tenth of China White there. He sported a smoking jacket, flip-flops, and a Cuban cigar. And, of course, at his side was the requisite model girlfriend. A willowy thing with the IQ of a tree. I wish I could take this opportunity to go against stereotype and portray for you an intelligent model. I cannot. She was a hampster. Her name was Fiona. She sat with

Arthur as he lorded over this mini-fortress, an enormous loft that was a paranoid's elegy to world domination where, to gain admittance, one had to ring buzzers and phones in a series of elaborately prearranged patterns.

I'd met Arthur through Jim, a punk bass player I'd taken up with not long after the Bug Scare. Jim was passionate and addicted to freebase. He had brought me with him to Arthur's one time, and while Jim was in the bathroom vacating his coke-loosened bowels, Arthur had slipped me a note with his various phone numbers on it.

I was by then an outright down-and-out skanky junkie chick. I was still remotely cute, but my arms were bruised and abscessed from shooting and my knees and shins were scraped from jumping off rooftops during raids. I'd nodded out at the recording studio so many times they'd sent me packing. I'd tried to have a life of crime. I was a cat burglar wracked with guilt over pilfering items from my neighbors' apartments. I'd climb down the fire escape, go in through a window, and take whatever was lying around. Then I would have the guilts for days. And so I ended up down on all fours, scooping hunks of pee-soaked litter out of Arthur's Abyssinian's box in hopes that he would give me free dope.

Which was what I was doing the day I met Jane. Hovering over the litter box, sneezing out my withdrawal symptoms. My hair, tinted burgundy, hung in a forelock down the middle of my face, obnubilating my vision of the bewildering world. I was depressed, having finally come to the conclusion that I was not only a bad burglar but a lousy junkie as well, this latter fact brought home to me by Nadine, a good junkie with whom I'd been keeping company lately. Nadine knew how to flip on five thousand volts of charm at the drop of a dime bag. She was half Cuban, half Jewish, and wore tight white clothing. When street dealers saw her coming, swinging her hips like a wrecking ball, they'd actually stand up straight and wipe the snot off their noses. And when Nadine hadn't been successful hustling guys at the strip club where she worked, she could certainly beg a bag off these slumbums. Not so with me. I lurched down the street in baggy pants and a smelly overcoat, looking like a strung-out boy with tits. Not *their* idea of a good time.

Where Nadine was the sort of girl to negotiate serious addiction with a minimum of suffering, I was clearly geared for maximum hell. I had to clean up after Arthur, the cat, and the model, who, incidently, would not fuck Arthur. This she frequently and volubly announced to anyone who would listen. And I suspect that demeaning cute junkie chicks was as close as Arthur got to sexual kicks.

As I stooped over my menial oeuvre, wheezing, sneezing, and inwardly whining to the heavens, the hells, and the souls of the dead, I heard footsteps coming toward the bathroom. This likely meant Arthur was coming to check on my progress. Fiona the Model was not around today and so Arthur had free rein to torture me and get off on it. He would probably sadistically dangle a Baggie of dope before my nose: FASTER, PUSSYCAT, SCRUB, SCRUB. Then, maybe he'd take a moment to expound upon Proust. This was a favorite pastime when he'd reached a certain level of zombiedom. He'd start off quoting a chunk of poor Marcel but then quickly veer from rhapsodic praise to, "Ah, fuck Proust, Proust is pretentious." This said with a Queens accent and a slight speech impediment that turned the *r*'s into *l*'s and the *s*'s into *th*'s: "Ploutht is pletentiouth."

I burrowed the scooper deep into the amonia-stinking clay and tried to appear busy as the footsteps came closer. When I looked up, a girl was standing in the doorway.

"Do you need a hand?" she said.

I didn't know how to interpret this. Had Arthur sent her to spy on my progress? Was this a set-up? Would there be unspeakable brutalities of emotional sadism in store for me if I did not answer with a humble but definite "No"?

I saw nothing evil in her face, though. It was a wide but fine-boned face with verging-on-Asian eyes. From her head sprouted corkscrew black fronds of hair. Her lips were thin but gracefully curved, giving her a subtle beauty. She wore unimposing loose clothes. She was, I knew, married to Martin, one of Arthur's pet artistes who, having not only written a book but a book that detailed the lives of two enterprising heroin addicts, was high in the pecking order of people who warranted free heroin sans menial tasks.

"Uh. . ." I finally answered. "Sure."

The girl immediately got down on all fours and voraciously dug into the task, this in and of itself forging a bond between us.

"You're married to that writer guy, huh?" I said then. This with slight resentment that she, by dint of marriage, did not have to demean herself for free drugs.

"Yeah. Martin. You're Zoe?"

I nodded.

"I've seen you over here before. I'm Jane."

"Oh," I said, glad to have been noticed, since most of the time I felt like a transparent and meaningless flea.

"You really don't *have* to do that," I said as Jane scooped up a clump of wet stuff.

"No, it's okay, I don't mind," she said. Then, with a twinkly smile: "You really look bedraggled."

"Oh. Well. Yeah." She had me there. Bedraggled I was. Which is perhaps why I failed to hear Arthur coming. Suddenly, he was there, towering above us, weaving through the air, his equilibrium profoundly disturbed from smoking and lording over that afternoon's Sick Salon. A seizure of wrath pretzeled his pale face. "Jane," he barked, "put down that implement, that's Zoe's job. She's got to learn some discipline. How will she ever learn if you *help* her? Stop it *now*."

Before I'd had time to consider his use of the word *implement*, Arthur violently knocked the turd scooper out of Jane's paw. Jane winced. Arthur then very deliberately stood on my own hand, which was pressed palm down against the floor. "Owwwww," I wailed, this a protest against the tortures of dope sickness as much as Arthur's foot grinding into the tiny bones of my hand. "That *hurts*," I said.

"That's not all that's gonna hurt," Arthur hissed. This was unlike him. Arthur was a creep, but usually not a physically violent creep.

As Arthur raised the litter scooper over his head, to *bash* me with its perforated plastic basket, Jane's husband, Martin, came walking into the bathroom.

"Arthur, what's going on here?" Martin demanded. He stood in front of Jane protectively and puffed himself up, this a failed attempt at looking imposing. He was every inch the writer type. Little glasses at the end of his nose, keen dark eyes, balding, thin, and dressed in worn cotton clothes.

Arthur looked confused then. He was far beyond recognizable emotions and was instead subject to vague Neanderthalic shifts of mood. He now stood there, half naked, sweating, brandishing the scooper, a kaleidoscope of failed neuron connections distorting his face.

"Arthur, my man, this is not cool," Martin said, shaking his head sadly. Arthur's brows knit themselves into evil sweaters, and just when he seemed on the verge of a verbal breakthrough, there was a fierce pounding at the front door. The ominousness of this *thwunk thwunk* was compounded by the fact that knocking was strictly forbidden; one had to gain entrance via the aforementioned buzzes and calls.

We all skulked out of the bathroom and stood looking at the door. By now the other artistes who had come that day to watch Arthur flail and dispense free dope were gone. It was just us. And we stood like frozen action figures in various stages of physical distress.

More *thwunks* and then: "ARTHUR, OPEN THIS FUCKING DOOR."

Arthur's eyes went wild. He dropped the litter scooper and his whole body started flapping like a big broken wing. Jane and Martin and I stood motionless. Then the *thwonking* turned to hacking, and within a few seconds, the blade of an axe bit through the door.

Rather than alarming Arthur, the gash enraged him and wiped out any instinct for self-preservation. He ripped the door open and screamed, "WHATHA FUCK YA DOIN' TO MY DOOR?"

A tall man with red hair and an axe burst in. "Arthur, you fuck, you made my WIFE mop your floor," he howled. "My WIFE doesn't *do* floors. You're going to pay for this." He was waving the axe in an arc above his head. It was fluid movement. I actually had the thought: What a graceful arc this man is making with his axe.

Arthur was torn between rage and fear. "Gerald, I don't know what you're talking about, and, man, be careful with that thing." Arthur tried to take the axe away from Gerald.

"Get the fuck away from me, you cretinous sack of shit," Gerald sneered. He was taller and much beefier than Arthur. He shoved Arthur back, then put the axe to Arthur's left nostril.

Martin and Jane and I didn't want any axe blades in *our* noses and so stood completely still.

"I'm not gonna put up with your crap anymore," Gerald said, still pressing the blade to Arthur's nose. "You're a power-hungry little bastard."

"But I didn't do anything!" Arthur protested, trying to back his nose away from the blade.

"You made my wife mop your floor, Arthur. That was my ex-wife that you demeaned. The blonde? Janine? Bet you didn't know that now, did you?" He snarled, "You just thought she was some poor little bitch stuck mopping for a fix, but that's my ex-wife. "

Arthur looked at a loss. After all, he had a vast stable of women mopping for a fix. I was just one of many, and so was this guy's ex-wife.

"I don't know anything about it. I don't know your wife, Gerald," Arthur protested. Then, with the kind of fluid speed I didn't suspect ailing Arthur had in him, he ducked the axe, spun around, and swiftly fished a gun out from under a couch pillow.

What had seemed like an almost playful scene, one that might end with some backslapping and an exchange of powders, had now turned deadly. Gerald tried to get the gun out of Arthur's hand. They wrestled. The gun went off. A quick blast muffled at once in flesh.

"Oh my fucking God, there's a hole in my hand," Arthur wailed, clutching his hand and turning green. There was indeed a hole in his hand. And he had put it there. Shot his own hand.

Next thing I knew, Martin was pulling on me, trying to get Jane and me out of there. Arthur leapt into our path, putting himself between us and the door: "Where you goin'? I've got a fuckin' *hole* in my hand, don't anybody move." Arthur waved his hand in our faces, its newlyformed bullet maw spitting blood like a gone consumption victim. Tall, willowy, skinny Martin puffed out his meager chest: "Hold it right there, Arthur, this has gone too far. We're leaving. Don't try to stop us."

"Zoe," Arthur wailed then, sticking his hand hole in my face, "you're going to LEAVE, too? You can't LEAVE ME, ZOE, you're SICK, you have to stay and help me, Zoe, help me."

I felt a twinge. Some demonic allegiance to Arthur and an enormous allegiance to every cell of my junkie being that loudly clamored: FEED ME FEED ME FEED ME.

But Martin and Jane yanked me out the door. We raced out onto the street, leaving Arthur and Gerald to battle it out. We hailed a cab and Martin breathlessly ordered the driver to drive.

For a few seconds we were all quiet. I was sicker and sicker by the minute. I had no money and nothing left to sell.

"Would you like to come over for tea?" Martin said then, breaking the silence. This was probably the most shocking thing he could have said to me at that moment. We had just survived an axe debacle at a dope dealer's house, I was dope sick, we were dope fiends, *tea?*

"Who, me?" I asked.

Martin laughed. I wasn't joking. The idea of tea was as alien to me as clean socks. Or any socks. I didn't have socks. And I don't think I'd ever had tea. Coffee, sure, but even that only to boost a speed head. Tea was alien. Tea was another world. I lived, by now, on Pitt Street. Pitt Street was just as it sounds. Pitty. Probably *nobody* on Pitt Street had tea. Even my lone friend, Nadine, for all her hip-swerving savvy, probably never had tea.

All the same, I accepted this invitation and soon the cab had pulled up in front of a West Nineteenth Street tenement building. We got out and climbed five flights up to Jane and Martin's cramped one-bedroom. I felt awkward and dope sick.

"Here, sit down," Jane said, gesturing toward a narrow red couch.

"You're sick?" Martin asked then, scrutinizing me from behind his little glasses.

"Oh, yes," I said, awkwardness banished by unmitigated need.

"I think I have a little something for you," Martin said, fishing a ball of tinfoil from his jacket pocket. "Our friend Arthur gets sloppy sometimes and drops things. Lucky for us, I pick them up." Martin produced a magnificent little rock of dope. My starved cells clamored and shifted.

As Martin cut a white line onto the nearest nonporous surface, I lost control, dropped to my knees, ripped the straw from his hand, and fiendishly vacuumed the stuff into my nostril. Martin refrained from chiding, "That was my line, you punk-ass savage." He smiled and offered the next line to Jane, who sniffed it as delicately as she appeared to do everything.

I could feel my cells feeding, the relief bathing me in a whirlpool of bliss. I sat back, letting the red couch suck me into its folds. Couches, like tea, were something I was no longer accustomed to. I lived most of my life on an enormous mattress. I was unfettered by dressers or couches. Most of the time, this pleased me. Occasionally, though, I harbored white-trash fantasies, and these all involved couches. There was a vague but warm future wherein I lived in a shack fifteen miles from a hick town. On my front lawn would be a dead couch and maybe the carcass of a car. My multitudinous smelly house pets would punctuate the yard with puke and shit. Near the lawn couch would be a little overhang built as shelter for the broken-down racehorse I'd saved from the glue factory. The horse would have a long, morose nose and, of course, a bum leg. I would have some chickens and maybe a goat. What I would do for money, I don't know. Sell eggs maybe. Make goat cheese.

Perhaps I'd be married, though. He'd be a motorcycle mechanic who worked on Harleys. He'd have a drinking problem, and although I'd have kicked dope, I'd still pop a lot of pills. There'd be a nasty-ass Dr. Feelgood on Main Street. I'd give him hand jobs and he'd write me

Valium and Percocet scripts. I'd nod out in the grocery store. Some sixteen-year-old grocery clerk would pick me up off the dairy case. He'd have acne but a fine physique. I'd let him give me a ride home to the shack. I'd invite him in for Valium and coffee. He'd go down on me. My husband the Harley mechanic would come in at that moment. Surly, drunk, his paunch punching the air before him. All hell would break loose. The acne-addled grocery clerk would high-tail it back to the Grand Union. My husband and I would throw couches at each other for two and a half hours, then get drunk and fuck. Then I'd go out and feed the chickens.

This was loosely the fantasy. It started out pleasantly enough but always ended in a debacle of polyester and drunkenness. For the time being, though, I was at ease, half nodding off on my new friends' couch.

As they puttered, Martin fixing a cheese platter while Jane, in a post-sniff bout of productivity, tidied the desk area, I took in the surroundings. The walls were lined with books. There were plants, candles, and a lush rug. There was a doddering calico cat. I closed my eyes for a while, then opened them when I heard the clacking of typewriter keys. Martin had settled behind the desk and was stuffing bits of cheese into his maw with one hand while typing with the other. I don't know how he had the appetite for cheese after ingesting Arthur's sublimely pure dope.

"Hey, sorry to be rude," Martin said. "Gotta get this done, though. We need the money. Otherwise it's another trip to Arthur's den of horrors."

"Oh, you're writing another novel?" I asked.

"Oh no, no, I'm writing another fuck book: 'He throbbed, she quivered, they came'—two hundred pages of that."

"Oh . . . wow."

Jane came back into the room then. "How do you feel now?" she asked solicitously.

"Much better, thanks." I smiled into her pleasing face. It was not the face of a dope fiend, there were no crags or obvious demons. She turned and put her hand on Martin's shoulder. "Hon, you want me to take over yet?"

"Yeah, if you don't mind, precious, I'm drying up." Martin stood then and Jane took his place in front of the typewriter.

"Martin starts the books," Jane said, "then, when he gets tired of 'he throbbed she quivered,' I take over. We get out one every two weeks. Five hundred dollars a book. It doesn't take care of our habits, though, so we end up at Arthur's more often than we'd like."

"Doesn't everyone?" I asked. Jane laughed then. A discreet laugh. Jane gave the impression of having been raised by nuns. There was something incredibly contained about her. And, at the same time, a generosity of spirit. Jane was a sort of Joan of Arc on dope.

As Jane typed, Martin made and poured tea. I threw half the sugar bowl into my steaming cup, then gulped it down. Because I had been junk-sick for so long and then imbibed of Arthur's strong dope, the tea at once made a return trip from my empty belly. I rushed blindly toward what I assumed to be the bathroom but instead found myself before the kitchen sink, into which I promptly expurgated brown and yellow liquid.

This was a new low in my puking standards. And these were high. I had vomited everywhere. A few years earlier, when my friend Hope and I were still in the honeymoon of our first habits, we'd taken up sight-seeing. We had suddenly become upset with ourselves for never having seen things like the Met, the Empire State Building, MOMA, and the World Trade Center. Three or four weekends in a row, we dosed ourselves and went sight-seeing. And I threw up. It wasn't unpleasant; throwing up from dope is virtually refreshing. It comes quite suddenly—you spew, you feel better. You view Manhattan. You ogle fine art and architecture. You startle the German tourists.

I also vomited on Philip Glass's shoe. It is inadvisable to do too much heroin and then go see Philip Glass. The music built in fervor, its repetitive progressions swerving and skirling majestically, causing my head to spin. I felt supremely nauseated but swallowed fiercely, trying to keep my Twinkie dinner down. I managed to hold it until the concert was finished. Then, as Philip Glass left the stage, I stood up to find the bathroom, but this motion made it come rushing out of me. I spewed onto the floor and some got on Philip Glass's shoe. He, however, was dazed from playing and didn't seem to notice this gaffe.

Now I was mortified at having puked on Jane and Martin's dishes. Jane, ever gracious, patted me on the back and showed me to the bathroom.

Here, I marveled at what I considered extreme plushness— a fuzzy bath mat, fluffed towels and soap, not a mere rank crust but a luscious pink thing that smelled of camellias. I rubbed the soap into a lather and scrubbed my face and hands. Ran my moist digits through my mauve hair. Then, worried that I'd left trails of dirt or slime in their beautiful bathroom, I started to inspect the sink. "Everything okay?" Jane called through the door. This startled me and the pink soap flew out of my paw and plonked into the toilet.

"Oh, sure, fine, I'm fine, thanks, I'll be out in a sec," I said, fishing the soap from the bowl. I rinsed it thoroughly, then emerged from the bathroom feeling close to presentable.

Jane and Martin were now the picture of domesticity. Martin stood looking over her shoulder as she scrolled through the newly typed page of porn. I knew it was time to leave. Although, of course, I did not want to. "Um, I guess I ought to go now," I said. They both turned to me, offering smiles tinged with relief. They were not, I could see, in the habit of baby-sitting grubby punk rock junkies. I was a curiosity and obviously a stray, but now they had given me a little TLC and they wanted to get back to their own thing.

"So, uh, I could call you guys sometime or something," I said then.

"Oh, please do," Jane said, scribbling their number down for me.

"Hey, listen, thanks a lot for getting me straight and everything, you know?"

"It's the least we could do," Martin said.

I turned and walked out. It had not occurred to me to clean my puke up out of their sink. Eight years later, Jane brought this up. We were vacationing together in Grenada. I had made a mess of our shared hotel room. She, with uncharacteristic force, chided me: "Zoe, you've got to pick up your crusties."

"My what?"

"Your underwear."

"My underwear isn't CRUSTY."

"Well, pick it up."

"Okay, okay, come on, we're on vacation."

"Yeah. Next you'll puke in the sink."

"Why would I do that?"

"You don't remember? The first time we met you you came over, nodded out on our couch, used all our sugar, and puked in the sink."

"Oh. I did? I puked in the sink?"

"Yes. You were a sub-dwarf."

"Well."

"Pick up your crusties."

I did.

I left Jane and Martin's and, as I walked all the way back to Pitt Street, wondered vaguely what was now transpiring at Arthur's and how he was negotiating the hole in his hand.

Back at the hovel, I lay on my vast mattress and stared at the wall for a while. Then, inspired by Martin and Jane's productivity, decided to write a novel. By hand, I began composing a tawdry tale of two punk rock junkie chicks who went sight-seeing. One of them puked a lot.

A few days went by. I talked to Jane, who told me Arthur had been in the hospital. She and Martin had gone to sit at his bedside, from whence, completely unfettered by the fact that he was in an institution, he doled out dope and coke as usual. He was, Jane said, more unbearable than ever. Fiona the Model had left him and he was being endlessly questioned by authorities for having shot a hole in his hand. And, she said, he had asked that I call. Which, of course, I did at once. I had, that afternoon, burglarized my downstairs neighbor, finding only a switchblade and some Valium. Then, wracked with the requisite guilt, I'd popped the Valium and, a little later, suceeded in translating the blade into two bags of dope. Now my resources were depleted.

When I called Arthur, he had just gotten back to his lair.

"ZOE, YOU DESERTED ME," he wailed into the phone.

"I'm sorry, Arthur," I groveled.

"Sorry, sorry, sorry. Yeah. Uh-huh. Yeah. Well. Come over. Get over here. Come over. Now. "

I was there in ten minutes. Rang the appropriate hidden buzzers. Climbed the stairs. Arthur stood near the patched door. His eyes were glazed and his head looked more swollen and melonlike than ever. He waved his holey hand at me. "I don't know why I'm even letting you come back, the way you deserted me, you left me with a HOLE IN MY HAND." I humbly lowered my traitor's eyes and made self-deprecating sounds. I saw that his hand was wrapped up in bandages but these were already lugubriously stained. Clearly Arthur had been home, smoking and snorting and popping, long enough to do damage to the hospital's handiwork.

I entered the lair. A girl was standing in the middle of the floor, looking elegant and smoking an ultra-long cigarette. I assumed she was a paying customer as opposed to a Menial Task Wench like me.

She extended a well-manicured hand at me, and said, with a thick French accent, "Allo, my name is Veronique, it is pleasure to meet you." She was wearing a creamy cashmere sweater and tailored pants. She smelled of something expensive.

"Yeah, yeah, yeah, Veronique, cut the civilities. That there is Zoe and she's a disloyal slut," Arthur said. "Zoe, meet Veronique, she thinks she's gonna get a free ride 'cause she's good-lookin'. WRONGO, Veronique!" At this, he laughed diabolically. "Now, you girls got your work cut out for you this evening. You be good little dope fiends and Daddy'll give you a fix. The faster you get the work done, the sooner I feed your habits." We followed him to the closet, where he showed us the implements of our doom. Brooms, mops, Spic and Span. He winked at us and suggested we make the floor feel like it'd had a tongue bath.

As we rolled up our sleeves and broached the task, Arthur reclined on the bed, stripped off his boxer shorts, and watched us through slit eyes as he alternately sucked on the base pipe and snorted lines of dope. I noticed that, perhaps as a result of waving his hand around to order us into action, his wound had started to ooze goo onto the bandage. I couldn't help but stare at it.

"Whadya lookin' at? MOP," he barked. I mopped. Veronique was down on all fours, scrubbing a stain.

A few minutes later, I looked up and saw Arthur nodding out. Some malevolent combination of dope, coke, and hand medication was putting even his highly tolerant system to the test. His chin kept bobbing down onto his chest, his jaw was slack, and his eyes had drooped shut. As he heaved sleepy breaths, the enormous Baggie of heroin that was lying on his stomach rose and fell to the rhythm of his nod.

Veronique and I stopped mopping and stared at the Baggie of heroin, and then, just as Veronique brazenly reached for the bag of bliss, Arthur's eyes popped open and went wild. He snatched her pretty French hand and twisted it in his good one.

"Owww," Veronique yowls.

"Arthur, stop!" I said.

"BOTH OF YOU SHUT UP!" Arthur screamed.

"FUKE YOU!" Veronique said, absurdly French.

"Fuke you" did not agree with Arthur. His face knotted. He fumbled for something in his bedside table, scattering papers, cigarettes, cassettes, and scraps of pot in his frenzy. Maybe he was looking for his gun. Maybe he was going to shoot holes in our hands, too. Just as I got ready to duck, Arthur's whole being loosened and he fell back and nodded out again. Just like that. One minute he was going to blow holes in us, the next, he was asleep.

Veronique and I eyeballed the Baggie, which was now resting just a few inches from Arthur's fingertips. As she moved to relieve him of it, Arthur came to once more: "All right, you two aren't doing any mopping, so why don't you fuck each other and then I'll give you some dope."

Veronique and I wrinkled up our noses at Arthur's desire to watch two junk-sick chicks go at it.

"Ooooo, how predictably *masculine* of you, Arthur," Veronique said tautly.

"Yeah," I said feebly.

"Yeah, yeah, yeah, predictable, sure, just shut up and do it."

Veronique and I considered each other for a few beats. One thing was clear: We needed dope. We both knew this. We approached each other and started to kiss. Her tongue tasted funny, sweet and incredibly feminine. It had never really occurred to me that tongues possessed gender-specific attributes. It wasn't disagreeable, but neither was it plunging me into a pool of desire. Our mutual ambivalence infuriated Arthur: "Dammit, come on, put some verve into it, hump each other, COME ON!"

Oh, what the hell. I dug my knee between her thighs and pushed her to the floor. She made an astonished O with her pretty French mouth. Then she smiled and pulled me on top of her. We ground crotches in a mock frenzy of passion. I yanked up her cashmere sweater, exposing smooth belly and a delicate lace push-up bra. Oh, God, tits, I thought. Now what? Veronique helped me out of that pinch. Pulled my hand onto her left breast, causing my little digits to grind into the pillowiness. Arthur started moaning while snorting lines and touching his lifeless dick.

Then, in an uncanny repeat sequence of the previous week's axe debacle, someone started pounding at the door. I took my hands off Veronique and stood up just as a booming voice said, "POLICE, OPEN UP!"

Arthur flew off the bed. "Take this," he said, hurling the bag of heroin at me. I dodged the dope, letting the Baggie land on the floor as a whole team of cops barged in the door.

They surrounded Arthur as Veronique and I stood by, trying to look innocent.

"Guy, why don't ya put some clothes on," one of the cops said, making a moue of disgust at the sight of naked Arthur. Arthur sputtered incomprehensibly but then obliged. One of the cops eyed Veronique and me but the rest did not seem interested in us. They had bigger fish to fry. There were about fifteen of them. Two in suits, the rest in blue. Shivers went down my back. I had never been busted. I'd burglarized, copped on the streets daily, gotten off in skanky shooting galleries that were raded two minutes after I left. Somehow I'd always been one step ahead of the ubiquitous NYPD blue. Now I was in their collective face.

The cops started searching the place, turning everything inside out. The suit cops were sitting with Arthur at the kitchen table. They were asking him stuff but I couldn't—and didn't really want—to hear what. I got the idea that it all went back to the guy with the axe. The guy with the axe I learned later on was a judge's son.

The uniformed cops found a few knives, the gun, a bag of pot, and one freebase rock, but, mysteriously, they failed to notice the *mountain* of heroin in a Baggie in the middle of the floor. They just didn't see it. They handcuffed Arthur. They said nothing to Veronique and I. Neither did Arthur. He shot us one filthy look before they led him out of the lair. It was the most unbelievable thing I'd ever seen. Once, when I was nineteen, I was having sex with a hippie guy in a sleazy hotel in San Francisco. Just as I was about to come, an earthquake rolled through the city. That was weird. This was weirder. They all left. Veronique and I stood frozen to our spots. I was sitting at the edge of Arthur's stained bed. Veronique was on a stool near the bookshelf. We were waiting for the cops or Arthur or *somebody* to notice they had left a mountain of pure heroin and two junk-sick junkies sitting in a room.

Apparently, no one noticed. After a few stunned minutes, Veronique said, "Oh, *mon Dieu*," in a lustful whisper, reverting to her native French. "*C'est incroyable.*"

"*Oui*," I said, staring at the bag of dope.

"*Alors?*" She cautiously walked over to the Baggie, as if maybe it was wired and would, at first touch, lick our faces in flames, or blow our heads off. "Want sum duhp?" she queried. She ogled the Baggie speculatively.

"It's not gonna blow up. Let's do it," I said, the Terminator of dope fiends. Veronique picked it up, stuck one long clean fingernail inside, and scooped a generous mound into her nose.

I put my entire *finger* in there, pulled it out caked with powder, and inhaled enormously. Veronique's own digit made another pass at the stuff. We began to gorge and feed, exacting our revenge on Arthur's Baggie. Eventually, it occurred to us to get out of there. The cops might come back, or, worse, Arthur. The mopping wouldn't be done and we'd have hoovered a noticeable portion of his dope. And he'd shoot us. He'd shoot our hands off and make us mop. We'd mop handless. With our toes. Or with our lips. We'd be smashed and we'd be mopping with our lips.

We decided to go to Veronique's, a plush loft in Tribeca. It was large and white. Although I was smashed, it occurred to me that I would probably smear dirt on the impeccable white couch she motioned for me to sit on. I sat at the very edge of the cushion and tried to act natural.

Veronique stood in the middle of the floor, weaving slightly, eyes at half mast. Behind her was a big thing of art. I don't know what else you would call it. It was a *thing*. A piece of wood protruding accusingly from the guts of a canvas. It was probably incredibly valuable, and I could not figure out why someone who had something like that had been demeaning herself, performing menial tasks for dope.

"All this is not mine," she said then, reading my thoughts. "Is my boyfriend's wife. She is in Zimbabwe now."

"Ah," I said.

"We spleet?"

"What's that?"

"We spleet the duhp?"

"Oh yes, absolutely, let's," I said.

She got another plastic Baggie from the kitchen and we divvied the goods into equal mounds. This took a while because we were loaded. Finally, she handed me my half, which I tucked into my underwear.

"You put it in panties?"

"Yeah."

"That's nice," she said, a perceptible lewd accent on the "nice." "You are not bad-looking, you know?" she added.

"Oh. Yeah, well, you, too," I said feebly.

She walked me to the door and kissed me lightly. "Don't eat all your bonbons at once," she warned. I would have keeled over blue and dead had I done even a twentieth of it at once.

I walked home to Pitt Street. Very slowly. The next day, I called on Jane and Martin. "Oh, " Jane said, opening the door, "you . . . um, you look very tired."

"Oh no, I feel *great*. And you will, too," I said, producing a little glassine bag of Arthur's dope.

Jane and Martin were hard-pressed to keep a cool exterior as I poured a pleasant mound of powder onto a cassette case. I regaled their junk cells, then told them the whole Veronique story. At first they refused to believe that Arthur could leave his dope behind. Even when getting hauled off to jail. Then, when I finally convinced them, Martin got worried: "I'd consider skipping town if I were you. Or maybe plastic surgery," he counseled. "Arthur's gonna be back in business before you can say 'Mop,' and he's going to find you."

This, somehow, had not occured to me.

The reality of it sank in when I arrived home many hours later. There hadn't been much in my apartment to begin with, but now there was truly nothing. Even my *mattress* had been removed by Arthur and his goons. The little door leading out onto the fire escape was banging in the breeze, a cool wind was blowing into my apartment. But there was nothing left to rustle.

A few weeks after this, I ended up in detox. Nadine, who at the urging of a new sugar daddy had cleaned up and found God, had contrived to get me a charity bed in a rehab. The place sat atop a hill in the middle of New Jersey and was a hot spot for junkie firemen and pill-popping teenagers. I spent five days in detox, aching, sneezing, and eating peanut butter, which for some reason alleviated withdrawal symptoms. I wore a bathrobe and paper slippers. The only person I spoke to was a fireman named Eddie who had at one time been a porn star. Eddie was about forty and this was his thirty-eighth rehab. One of the rehab counselors, thinking perhaps that Eddie and I were planning to run away from rehab, shack up, shoot dope, and die, ordered us not to speak to each other. Eddie was sent off to room with some other firemen and I was thrown in with seven girls, most of them bulemic as well as recovering from coke, dope, and pills. Diana, the girl with whom I shared a closet, was an extreme bulemic. Once, I went looking for something in our closet. I lifted up her suitcase and found dozens of plates with congealed food scraps under it.

The rehab didn't allow books or typewriters, but by hand I started to write a novel. It was about living with a bulemic who stashed plates of food in the closet and was prone to jumping up and down on her bed screaming, "I'M FAT, I'M FAT, KILL ME, I'M FAT."

I had trouble getting beyond the first chapter, though. One day, a letter came from Jane and Martin. It was full of amusing anecdotes about writing fuck books and going on the methadone program. Arthur, they informed me, had lost his lair and was now living with his mother in Queens. Jane and Martin were on methadone for a little while but planned to get clean.

Hearing from them inspired me to try my hand at my own fuck book. He throbbed, she quivered. Only I did it from the female perspective, so it was "She throbbed, he quivered." I worked whenever I had free time from attending self-help meetings and encounter groups and psychological evaluations. It became a twisted fuck book.

When, after a month, they released me from the rehab and sent me to a halfway house in Pennsylvania, I had finished the book. I sent it to Jane and Martin, who, with a few edits and corrections, were able to sell it. The day I checked into the halfway house, I was five hundred bucks richer and the oozing maw where I used to shoot up was healing over and scarring. My mother, Francine, and my father, Charlie, had, as a result of my ill whereabouts, spoken to each other for the first time in fifteen years. They had pooled together their modest funds to pay part of my way at the halfway house. This was as close to any sort of family feeling I'd had in a long time. They had coughed up some dough and each one called me there at the halfway house on the day of my arrival. It was sweet.

The halfway house had a sort of philosophy about breaking the spirit of us dope fiends: Make us perform menial tasks. And, where I had once scrubbed toilets for a fix, now I scrubbed them ostensibly to keep needles out of tender places.

It wasn't exactly my idea of a good time, but it had its perverted appeal. And that's all I've ever asked for in anything or anyone. Perverted appeal.

13

Dumped by the Devil, Fingered by His Doctor

Satan looked like he had plenty of perverted appeal. He looked like the kind of guy who would tie you up just right. He looked like he would tie you up and call you a slut as he fucked you slowly. Looks can be deceiving.

A few days after Satan dumped me, I happened to have an appointment for a physical. I was not in the best of spirits. A few things had gone severely wrong. Getting dumped by the devil was practically the least of it. But more on that later.

I went to see a guy named Dr. Harris, who had been recommended by Satan before he and I broke up.

Dr. Harris was attractive in an older, tidy kind of way. He was slight and his features were arranged nicely. When we shook hands, his paw lingered in mine a fraction of a second longer than was required. He splayed me out on the examining table, then commenced to poke and prod at me as if I were a giant gigot being trussed up for some frightening doctoral feast.

Then came the question game. Any history of heart disease? No. Good bowel movements? Why, yes, thank you. Then: "I need to feel your rectum."

"Oh," I said.

"Bear down like you're about to take a dump," he said. "It'll make it more pleasant."

"Ah," I said, "okay."

As Dr. Harris's tidy finger zoomed up my personal waste-evacuation system, he and I locked eyes there beneath the fluorescent light and an *erotic charge* shot through the air. He felt it, too. I could see he was jarred as he went to the sink to ostensibly rinse off his hands but in truth to quiet the raging boner I was certain must now be tenting his khaki pants.

When he turned back around, my eyes went to his crotch, but it looked fully composed. He asked a few more questions, then told me I was in fine physical form. We shook hands and I went home.

Later that day, I talked to Satan for the first time since the breakup. He wanted his chair back. A functioinal gray office chair he had loaned me for my fuck-book-writing comfort. That he dared, after ending things in a manner whose cruelty I will later recount for you in exacting detail, call and ask about his chair was a testament to the fact that he was, indeed, the devil. Just in case you thought this was a joke. A cute way to convey my minced emotions. Not so. The devil called to ask for his chair back. I took this opportunity to tell him about the doctor's erotic finger.

"Oh, yeah," Satan said, "Dr. Harris gave me a physical last week and he put his finger up my ass, too, and I'm sure he liked *my* ass better than *your* ass. He's totally gay."

"How do you know?"

"Because," Satan said, "the one guy I ever had sex with is now Dr. Harris's boyfriend. That's how I found Dr. Harris. He's the boyfriend of a guy that used to fuck me in the ass. So I'm sure Dr. Harris liked *my* ass, but I doubt *your* ass did much for him."

I hung up. This exchange basically summarized our relationship. We were in constant competition: whose ass would be more of a turn-on in a rectal exam.

Now, for all his crimes, for stealing me away from Bev, for being boring in bed but making me love him and then dumping me, for all this, Satan is going to have to pay. Which is why I am going to go out, get a gun, call my best friend, Jane, then, at gunpoint, make him perform menial tasks. I can't wait.

14

Humping Hilda

The halfway house was called, dubiously enough, House of Winners. It was located in what had formerly been the psych ward of a hospital. The ceilings were high and the halls were wide. Rooms that had formerly been used for obscure psychiatric experiments had been converted into sleeping quarters replete with bunk beds. There were sixteen of us there at House of Winners and we all had to room with at least one person. I got paired off with yet another bulimic by the name of Diana. Diana was a fastidious snot. She kept all her clothes in impeccable order. She kept her hair in impeccable order. She wore pressed designer jeans and pink shirts. And I was a slovenly sub-dwarf, scarred and charred, my long purple mop now lopped off into a natural brown crew cut. Diana was the clean-cut speed freak. I was the lugubrious punk dope fiend. We spoke infrequently.

Mike, a handsome hard-core dope fiend who was in the halfway house for the seventeenth time, befriended me. Mike was pushing forty, had been a fireman, a cop, a factory worker, and, most recently, a burglar. Mike liked to pump iron and, as a vague sort of seduction attempt, I one day asked him to instruct me in this art.

We were in his room, pumping iron, when we were found by Michelle, the female counselor. Just as Mike put his hand on my bicep to see how well I was executing a curl, Michelle pounced into the room. "What's going on in here?" she demanded, eyes popping, body jiggling, adrenalized at the the possibility of catching two inmates engaged in anything remotely sexual.

Mike and I stood there stupidly as Michelle put her hands on her hips and admonished, "Zoe, you know the rules, what are you doing in Mike's room?" Her eyes narrowed and sank into the pockets of fat that punctuated her cheeks.

"He was just showing me how to do curls, Michelle."

"Michelle, I'm so sorry, I was just showing Zoe some exercises, I didn't mean to break any rules," Mike groveled.

"Umfff," Michelle snorted. "Zoe, you come along with me. I've got some chores for you "

And so I begrudgingly followed Michelle to the broom closet, from whence she produced a toilet scrub brush and cleanser. She sent me off to scrub for salvation.

About an hour into my ouevre, as I flicked the last speck of fudge from the toilet's maw, Michelle came in the bathroom, put her hands on her hips, and gestured at a faint pee streak beneath the rim of the toilet seat .

"What's *that*?" she demanded.

"Uh, I dunno, lemon juice."

"Watch your mouth, Zoe, your attitude's gonna get you high," she said.

"Uh-huh," I muttered.

"Don't you 'uh-huh' me," she said, her thin lip curling up to reveal a row of impossibly tiny teeth. "I've had about enough of this attitude of yours," she spat, attacking my fragile ego structure with the rusted fork of her banality. "I think if you're sober enough to be a snot, you're sober enough to go get a job."

And so, the next day, with my youth and my post-punk detox good looks on my side, I pounded the pavement, and, after answering a half dozen dreary Help Wanted ads, I got myself a job at a cardboard box factory. They hired me on the spot, and after a half-hour training session, I stood at the end of a conveyor belt, catching and folding flaps of cardboard. My fellow cardboard workers were two speed-freak skinheads who took pleasure in feeding boxes into the machine so fast the flaps flew in my face and I repeatedly lost control, fell backward, and got cardboard dust stuck in my crew cut.

By the end of the day, I stank of cardboard and I wanted to shoot dope.

I trudged home to the halfway house and sat in the communal lounge area picking at the welfare office's cheese food product. I made cheese balls and played marbles with them. This was what it had come to. Just as I contemplated sticking my head in the oven and baking myself, a boy teetered into the room, stood wobbling for a moment, then fell into a chair. He was, I supposed, a new candidate for rehabilitation through scrubbing. He was also apparently still in the wobbles of his last drunk. He was blond and very young. He wore an ACDC T-shirt.

After a while, he looked up, noticed me, smiled crookedly, and said, "Hi, I'm Robbie."

"Hi, Robbie, I'm Zoe," I said soberly, my desire to live instantly reinstated. Then snatched away once more as Michelle barged in, whisked Robbie away, and ordered me to go attend a self-help meeting at the nearby Salvation Army.

The self-help meeting was mostly made up of compulsive gamblers in trenchcoats. A few housefraus with hairspray habits. I sat in the back and napped. When the meeting ended, the whole lot of them stood up, held hands, and praised God. I then noticed her, wedged between a pair of hefty housewives, a girl close to my age who, for some obscure reason, magnetized me. She was big as a house and wore pale blue overalls and army boots. She had a terrible case of acne. She looked bedraggled, confused, and sad. I decided to introduce myself.

She winced as I approached, fearing, I suppose, that I would try to hug her or tell her Jesus is her friend.

"Hi, I'm Zoe," I said, extending my hand. She knit her pale brows, made a slight O with her lips, then said, "Hi, I'm Hilda."

Hilda was detoxing from a Valium habit. She was also schizophrenic. But stabilizing. And, having recently lost her job as a French fry cook at McDonald's, she was looking for work.

The next day, I got Hilda a job at the box factory, too. Mr. Peets, the box factory manager, generously paired us off and we became a dream team. She fed the machine, I caught and folded the flaps. Hilda in motion was a graceful box-making goddess, she was seamless, smooth, orchestrated.

As our skinhead coworkers sneered in our general direction, Mr. Peets looked on, pleased at our productivity. A few days went by in this fashion as Hilda and I zipped through our shift and at night skulked off to the Salvation Army, where we sat in the back of the self-help meetings, sneering and listening for good anecdotes. Now that I was employed, Michelle the Rehab Counselor was blissfully off my metaphoric dick. Life was better.

One day at lunch break, Hilda and I went out to sit in her car. Hilda, who had since childhood harbored an enormous Keith Richards fixation, was blasting a tape she had made of all the Rolling Stones' Keith-sung songs.

"Come on, Hilda, can't we listen to the Sex Pistols, please?" I implored, producing the cassette of *Never Mind the Bullocks* that I carried with me at all times.

Hilda wouldn't go for it. "No way," she said. "Get away from me with that Sex Pistols stuff, my therapist says punk rock makes me do downers."

"Oh," I said.

We ate lunch as Keith Richards sang about love. Hilda whipped out a salami, Cheez Doodles, a big bag of M&M's, and thirty-two ounces of Diet Coke. Then, to my horror, she produced a joint. Not a mere joint this, but a fat stubby thing, the delicious stink of which was overpowering the salami smell. Hilda turned on a wicked smile and said, "Dessert."

My eyes grew saucer-sized. My whole being ached for this fat little cigarette. Conversely, my fear of Michelle the Counselor was huge and repressive. Were she to find me out, I'd be expelled on my punk ass. And I had nowhere to go and approximately seventeen dollars to my name.

But Hilda kept taunting me: "Oooh, come on, Zoe, it's gonna feel soooo nice, you're gonna get so fucked up, your head's gonna spin right off your shoulders."

Ah. Yes. I relented. "Okay, I'll make a deal with you. We listen to the Pistols and then I'll get stoned with you." Hilda went along with this, and as "Holidays in the Sun" thundered through the Nova's crackly speakers, Hilda fired up. I had taken only two hits before the Mack truck of paranoia came flying at me. My system was, after all, squeaky clean, and now the THC was having its way with my depth perception and motor coordination. Which all served to enlarge Hilda's already meaty face as she, apparently possessed by evil gods of weed, yanked me to her and commenced to *lick* my mouth.

Sometimes the grotesque is incredibly erotic. This was one of those times. Now, as Hilda pulled back for a second, I noticed orange Cheez Doodle crust stuck on the side of her mouth. I felt a wave of nausea and exhilaration. And I went for it. I mushed my hand into her huge thigh, licked the Cheez Doodle crumbs from her lips, and heaved an enormous sigh. As the last chords of "Anarchy in the U.K." faded out, as Hilda's tongue traveled at Warp Nine from the tip of my chin down the modest cleavage of my T-shirt, just then, Mr. Peets, Box Factory Manager, pressed his face against the steamed-up car window.

And what a sight it must have been: two red-eyed same-gendered cardboard workers humping through a cloud of pot smoke. Mr. Peets's face turned beet red. He made O shapes with his mouth but no sounds came out. He slowly backed away from the car.

Hilda and I stopped humping, straightened out our frumped-up clothing, and returned to our workstations. No one at the factory said a word to us.

The next morning, we found pink slips in our pay envelopes. This sent Hilda into a fit of low self-esteem, and I could see her zit population quadrupling as we stood there, pink slips in hand.

Hilda went home to cry into a salami. I went to pound the pavement. Within two days, I got hired on for the graveyard shift at a screw factory. They didn't actually manufacture screws, but my job was to use a tiny screwdriver and screw miniature screws into little metal plates.

One night, Hilda came to visit me on my three A.M. lunch break. We went out behind the factory and sat by a toxic pond. It was cold and quiet there. There was the smell of decay and burning plastic. The ink of the sky had a slightly orange hue. Just as a big metal pipe belched waste material into the pond, I put my hand on Hilda's thigh. To my dismay, the formerly horny Hilda started to cry. Huge Hilda tears streamed down her face.

"Hilda, Hilda, what's wrong?"

"Well, I . . ." *Snarf.* "I stopped taking my medication and now I'm all moody and stuff and I—" *Snarf.* "Don't take it personal or anything, but I don't have any sex drive left and . . . PLEASE DON'T TOUCH ME."

I was mortified. I took my hand off her thigh and for a few moments sat in complete silence. Hilda was still weeping. After a while, I gingerly took her elbow and steered her back to the parking lot. She got into her car and drove away without another word. Goodbye, Hilda.

I returned to my workstation and furiously drove screws into the little metal plates. One of my coworkers offered me a hit of speed, but my pot experience with Hilda had proven too rich for my blood. The combined effects of the rehab, the halfway house, the toilets, and the self-help meetings at the Salvation Army had on some level worked their trick. I was afraid of what I'd turn into. They had truly and successfully convinced me that one hit of speed would eventually lead me back to needles, abscesses, poverty, and despair. I screwed the metal plates uninebriated.

Dawn came, sending a filter of light through the grimed factory windows. At seven A.M. I punched out and caught the bus home to the halfway house. I trudged through the door, tired, smelly, and horny. No sooner had I set foot in the place than Michelle, who was just coming on duty, intercepted me, handed me some toilet tools, and sent me off to scrub the immense third-floor bathroom. This to burn off demerits I'd earned for being surly in group therapy a day earlier.

Soon I was down on all fours communing with filth. It was at this moment that a full awareness of the human condition came to me: I am alone and I am scrubbing, so it is, and so it shall be. No matter how glorified a toilet I may one day scrub, still I will be scrubbing, I will be removing flecks of fudge from inside a bowl. And I will be alone. This illumination depressed me. Tears came. I was crying and scrubbing. And I needed, quite simply, a fuck. They were always telling us to pray. I was already on all fours, humbled to the bone. I turned my face toward the ceiling and said: "Dear Universe, please let me have sex and I will do whatever you want. I mean it."

The bathroom door opened. A crescent of brightness shone onto the filthy bathroom floor and there, his face made radiant by the fluorescent hallway light, there stood Robbie, the teenage alcoholic who had been admitted the previous week.

"Michelle said to bring you this," he drawled, handing me a jug of blue toilet-bowl cleaner.

"Thank you," I said softly. I looked into his pale eyes and saw something steaming there. Then, as I reached for the blue shit, our fingers entwined around the bottle and we both started to squeeze. My breath caught in my throat. Robbie's heartbeat began pumping through the thin fabric of his Metallica T-shirt. As he pressed his mouth to mine, we both squeezed the toilet cleaner bottle that we were still clutching like some odd totem to our budding industrial-strength lust. In a jerk of passion, Robbie squeezed the thing too hard. The top popped off and blue shit oozed out and puddled on the floor. I grabbed at the back of Robbie's ill-fitting pants, digging for his thin pancake ass. In doing so, I lost my balance, slid on the blue puddle, and landed ass first on the floor.

Robbie threw himself on top of me and started humping my thigh. We ripped off our clothes and were soon pretzeled and going at it, releasing our pent-up sober passions. What transpired next was what both Robbie and I later came to think of as the "spiritual awakening" we were being endlessly nagged to have. We came, together and blindingly, our asses smeared in toilet cleaner. The power of this orgasm was such that it seemed reasonable to forever renounce the booze and dope if this was the payoff.

Fucking on the bathroom floor kept us sober.

This was our first and last bout, though, for Robbie was sent back to his parents a few days later. I persevered at the screw factory a while longer and then, when I was deemed, if not a potential participant in society and its acts, then at least not a threat to myself and those around me, I was discharged from the halfway house. I left with a snarl and a check for two hundred dollars that Martin and Jane had gotten for me when I'd turned Robbie's and my spiritual awakening into an erotic story.

I made plans to fly out to Colorado, where my mother, Francine, was living. Francine had graciously allowed that I could move into her basement while I got my post–halfway house ass in gear.

The day before leaving Pennsylvania, as I was walking out of Woolworth's, where I'd bought some red hair dye, I ran into Hilda. She was walking hand in hand with a gnarly bull dyke. This was brazen of her since Scranton, PA, was not reknown for its homo-friendly feelings.

"Oh, hi," Hilda said, seeing me.

"Hi, Hilda, how's it going?"

"Good, really good. This is my girlfriend Wendy. We're getting married."

"Oh, cool. Hi, Wendy, nice to meet you." I shook the girl's stump of a paw. Wendy smirked. Hilda beamed. A few pleasantries passed among us all and then I skulked off, musing that Hilda's sex drive had apparently come back and that all had worked out in the end. Hilda was getting some, I had gotten some, Robbie had gotten some. Michelle had a new influx of souls to be saved through scrubbing. Yes. All was well.

And so I moved to Colorado and became a dishwasher.

15

Faster, Satan, Scrub, Scrub

We're getting close to the end. The end of the blueprint for my emotional idiocy. Do you see now? Is it at all clear? Can you begin to fathom how it is that I am sitting in my ex-boyfriend's closet with a bicycle chain in my lap? Do you understand that I know this is ridiculous but I cannot, and do not, want to help it? This is my reality, kids. Read it and weep till your eyeballs pop out and bounce down the crooked steps of my soul.

I like the idea of bringing Jane in on this. She will come over to help me hold Satan at gunpoint while he scrubs toilets. Maybe I will also invite Elizabeth, Oliver, and my friend Beth. We will be a fierce quintet holding the devil at gunpoint. I know that Beth would really get a lot out of it. Beth has endlessly ended up with psycho boys. Boys who like knives and pain. And I can imagine her giggling, a sadistic fire in her eyes, a gun in her hand: Faster, Satan, scrub, scrub. But Beth is broke right now. And I am also poor right now. If I could, though, I would fly her from Milwaukee to come take part in this sadistic quintet. For we are close now. We were not close for a while. Now, since Beth's last visit, we are close once more. And so I would like to bring her in on the fun. I want all the people I love to be here with me as I torture the devil.

16

Mortal Combat

I first met Beth during the dishwasher phase that followed the halfway house/box factory phase. I worked at a Buddhist café in Boulder, Colorado. I was twenty-three. I had a crew cut and many earrings. I was living in my mother's basement. I was having trouble writing fuck books. I had had the notion that fuck book writing was to be my career. I would, I thought, sit there at my mother's, whipping them out, send them off to Jane and Martin, build a healthy savings account, and move back to New York. But I couldn't seem to do much of anything, never mind write fuck books. So I got a job bussing tables and washing dishes at the Spear Café. My boss was a thin Buddhist named Will. He was pale and very tense. His face was like an illustration of the Buddhist precept "All life is suffering." He seldom smiled and hated the hippies and layabout poets who frequented the Spear Café. Because I had promptly fallen deeply in love with Will, I hated the hippies and poets by association.

Whenever Will and I were alone in the coffee storage room, I thought of grabbing him. Or, to be more exact, I thought of him grabbing me, throwing me down on a sack of coffee beans, and showing me the full meaning of "All life is suffering." Will never picked up on this desire, the metaphoric molecules of which so obviously thickened the air between us. Or maybe he did. He was married and had kids, and presumably part of "All life is suffering" was that you didn't fool around with punk rock dishwashers. But I loved him and did my best to hate everyone he hated. The hippies were easy to hate. They bought one eighty-cent cup of coffee, shared it among five people, and sat around the café all day, smoking clove cigarettes and talking about Jerry and the Dead. The poets were harder to hate. They were, compared to the hippies, big spenders and would each buy a beverage before sitting for hours dissecting Rimbaud, Iggy Pop, and Gregory Corso. They often smuggled booze in and as they drank it would grow increasingly boisterous and *outre* in their loud proclamations on the nature of art, love, and drugs. There were about ten of them. Mostly boys in their late twenties. Some were older or younger, and there were a few women, Fatima, a Portuguese photographer who was shacking up with Rick the Poet, and Beth, a diminutive and fiery-looking poetess. Beth was under five feet and weighed about seventy pounds. I knew her name because, in spite of Will's hatred of them, I studied and eavesdropped on the poets as they sat there all day, loafing and quipping. They seemed to be having a good time. They all seemed to fuck one another and make art about it. It was sort of like Paris in the twenties. Or so I imagined.

Beth was the most interesting to watch. She had a feline face with green eyes that caught light and threw it back at you. She seemed to listen more than talk. This I liked. A few times I saw her eyeballing me speculatively. Which made me nervous. Although I was curious about the poets, I was afraid to talk to them. I didn't have a lot of social skills.

Then one day Heddy the Bodybuilder took a liking to me, took it upon herself to socialize with me, which inadvertently led to Beth's and my eventual friendship. Heddy was a short, stocky girl with muscles and tattoos. She spent a lot of time in the café, scribbling madly on yellow legal pads. I didn't hate her. She wasn't a hippie. She bought not one but at least three cups of coffee. And she was truly weird-looking. She had shaved off her eyebrows and some days penciled them back on, but other days went *au naturel*. Her hair was bottle-black with red roots. And she had a slight but noticeable mustache. Every time I cleared away one of her cups she smiled at me. Eventually this evolved into actual dialogue, and before long, Heddy had convinced me to hang out with her.

I agreed to go to the movies with Heddy and some other girls she knew. Heddy, it transpired, was a recovering drunkard and so were her friends, Fran and Leah. Heddy was duly impressed that I had been a cat burglar/dope fiend. I rated. Heddy told me she was trying to write a self-help book. This is what she was doing in the Spear Café when I saw her scribbling. Authoring her first tome: *Self-Help for Cynics*.

One night I met Heddy and her friends and we went to see *Sid and Nancy*. The friends were as weird as Heddy. There was Fran, a petite, dykey-looking girl. She was a lesbian who was married with two kids. For a while she'd thought herself hetero. Now that she was sober, she realized she was lesbo and was accordingly having an affair with a diesel dyke with a fat ass. About two sentences into our first conversation, as we waited in line for popcorn, Fran said, "I like chicks with fat asses. What can I say."

Leah was a yuppie gone wrong. At first glance, she just looked like a yuppie. At second glance, there was something too crazy in her eyes. Leah was studying for her MBA, because, of her own admission, her goal in life was to become an astute businesswoman, own some condos, find a nice boy with a big dick and a bigger checkbook, and someday pop out some kids. She unabashedly wore pink and beige and went skiing in Aspen whenever possible.

We four had fun at *Sid and Nancy*. We stuffed our faces with popcorn. I cried when Sid died. Leah reverently asked me, "Do you know people like that in New York?" gesturing at the bedraggled junkies and punks on-screen. When I nodded that yes, I did, I won points with Leah. She wanted to slum vicariously through me.

From that night on, I spent a fair amount of time with those girls. We'd go to movies. Or just sit somewhere and talk about sex or about whoever was walking by. We called ourselves the Old Sluts Club, even though none of us was over twenty-eight and I for one hadn't had sex since Robbie the Teenage Alcoholic. Still, we liked to think of ourselves as the Old Sluts Club.

Sometimes, the Old Sluts Club would go to the Spear Café to hang out. At first this made me nervous, to hang out where I worked. But I adjusted. One night we were there at the same time as the poets. We were being loud. Fran was going on and on about how her girlfriend had gained twenty pounds and had *two* asses now. I caught Beth the Poet eyeballing me.

I ventured a smile. Beth smiled back and gestured for me to come over to the poets' table.

"Your friend has a big mouth," she said as I came to stand near her.

"Oh . . . uh . . . yeah, I guess," I said, hesitantly sitting down. "She, uh . . . she likes to talk about asses."

"Yes, I gathered as much. Why are you so tense all the time?"

"What?" Shorty here was getting awfully intimate. I winced a little. She patted my hand. "Don't take it the wrong way. I mean it in the nicest way possible." The other poets were eyeballing me now. They all knew me as the Angry Dishwasher. They'd seen me chewing the hippies out as I furiously swiped away their clove ashes. Some of them had seen me read an excerpt from my latest attempted fuck book at an open reading a few days earlier.

"You're the tensest dishwasher alive," Beth said then. "Maybe you should look into meditation."

"Uh . . . Well, uh, yeah, I guess," I said queasily.

"Give me your back."

"What?"

"Turn around, I'll give you a back rub. I'm studying to be a massage therapist." My lip curled into a sort of snarl. Beth at once snarled back at me: "Just turn around. I'm not being New Age, it'll be good for you." And so I let Beth dig her tiny but strong digits into my knots. As she did this, I looked over at Fran, who was still discoursing on her girlfriend's additional ass. Fran caught my eye and gave me a significant wink. She apparently thought Beth's back rub a prelude to gay sex. Beth rubbed for a while, and when she had noticeably loosened my back, introduced me to the other poets. First there was Kendrick, who seemed to be their unofficial leader. Kendrick was all shoulders, eyes, and popping veins. His hair was blondish and knotted into involuntary dreadlocks, and he had a sort of wild-beast look to him, which in part explained why, from what I'd heard, nearly every woman in the city of Boulder had fucked him or wanted to fuck him. Much to the chagrin of Peter, another of the poets. Peter was obsessed with Jack Kerouac and thought he was Iggy Pop. Although Peter was technically better-looking than Kendrick, he was not as appealing. Peter, when Beth introduced me to Peter, flapped his pretty eyes at me, then turned back to Rick the Rotund Poet, with whom he was discussing the poetry of Mayakovski. Rick merely grunted when Beth introduced me.

"We're going camping tomorrow," Beth said, motioning to the rest of the poets. "You should come with us. You, too, Andrew," she said as Andrew, an older poet who'd actually published books, pulled up a chair and sat down. Andrew looked like a factory worker. He was thick, wore Buddy Holly glasses and work shirts and always carried a beer. He wrote beautiful poetry about love and war. This I knew because, the first time I'd seen Andrew, I'd thought him sexy and immediately went out and bought copies of his books. Now Andrew grunted a "maybe" at Beth's camping invitation, then started talking to Scotty the Language Poet.

"You really should come with us, Zoe," Beth said then, "it'll be relaxing. Scotty's got a van, we'll all pile in then spend the night up in the mountains." I don't know how she knew my name. The whole situation was making me nervous and I noticed that the Old Sluts Club were ready to leave the Spear Café. I told Beth that yes, maybe I'd come camping. We exchanged numbers then the sluts and I left the café. The sluts teased me about the camping invite. "Yup," said Fran, "this time tomorrow, you gonna be munching some RUG!" She laughed so hard I thought she would break.

Although I did not plan to munch Beth's rug, I thought I probably would go camping with the poets. It would, after all, get me out of the house. My mother, Francine, was driving me nuts. Whenever I lurked around at home, she'd sick me with household chores. She thought this was the least I could do in exchange for living in her basement. She had a point. But it seemed that everywhere I went there was a toilet waiting to be scrubbed. And I'd had enough. I was desperately hording my modest dishwasher wages so that I could move out of my mother's and never clean toilets again. To this day, I don't do toilets. A few years ago, when I sold three fuck books in one month and accordingly felt RICH, I hired a maid. It's true. I now live next door to someone called Eye Guy. I often cannot afford my rent. But I have a maid. I don't look like the kind of girl who has a maid. If you saw me on the street, you wouldn't go, "Hey, that little bitch has a maid." No. I look like I either do my own cleaning or else live in *dirt*. But I don't. I have a maid named Betty. She drives me insane by re-arranging my stuff when all I want is for her to *scrub*. But she works cheap. And I am exploiting her. She is a former hippie past her prime. She goes to botanical school. She has six dogs, a parakeet, and three cats. She has to be my maid to support her pet habit. Which is good for me. Otherwise, I'd be buried in dirt. I'm a slob. The Reader is a slob. Satan, of course, was incredibly anal and tidy. Bev was a worse slob than me. Had Bev and I stayed together, we would have ultimately buried each other in dirtballs, hair, and ashes. One day Eye Guy would have smelled a horrible stench and come in to find me and Bev dead and buried in each other's dirt.

Beth is not a slob. When she and I were eventually roommates, I drove her crazy. I had a cat with long white fur. My cat left fur balls in Beth's stuff while I trailed ashes, gum wads, and crumbs all over the house.

Jane, my best friend in the world, is also tidy. She thinks I'm less of a slob now than when she first met me, when we were both junkies. She was a tidy junkie, I was a messy junkie. I would go over to her and Martin's house, lie about on the couch, and when I got up, there would be a moat of crumbs, bloody cotton balls, ashes, dirt, and hair surrounding the spot where my ass had been.

So. My mother was making me clean and I needed to accept any and all invitations to get out of the house. Accordingly, I did go camping with Beth and the poets. We all piled into Scotty's van. Kendrick wanted to go to Estes Park, but the others thought driving a few miles up the nearest mountain road would suffice. We drove for a little while and then Rotund Rick's girlfriend, Fatima, had to pee. She went off into some trees to take care of business. Scotty got out, looked around, and announced that we had driven far enough. We would camp in this spot.

"Scotty, no, this is absurd," Kendrick said. "We need a wilderness experience. This is lame, we can't even get naked here, too many people come around."

"Ha," Scotty said and at once took off all his clothes. Not one to be outdone, Kendrick also divested himself. Scotty and Kendrick then started to drink. Just sat down, naked, and drank. The others, some partially naked, some fully clothed, followed suit. Only Beth was not drinking. She and I sat on a rock.

"I can't drink, I just throw up. I'm too tiny. It rips through me, then comes out both ends," Beth said.

"Yeah, I don't drink either. I used to be a big dope fiend and then I got locked away in rehabs and stuff and they brainwashed me, so now I'm convinced if I do so much as have a sip of beer, I'll like kill my mother, eat the family dog, and fuck the pope all in one night."

"The pope would probably hate that," Beth said.

As the night thickened, as Beth made eyes at Kendrick and I made eyes at Andrew, and as the others drank themselves to a twirling and blurring oblivion and howled poetry at the moon, Beth and I bonded.

By dawn almost everyone had fucked each other and passed out. Kendrick had finally started kissing Beth but had gotten nauseous in the middle of a grope and had to go lie down. Rick and Fatima were lying entwined, using their last energies to pour beer into each other. This a sort of reconciliation after Rick had found Fatima going down on Scotty. Andrew, who for a while had been cruising Scotty's girlfriend, at last turned his attentions to me.

"Sun's gonna come up, huh?" he said.

"Yup, guess so," I said, trying to think of something poetic and/or sexy to say.

"You look like a New York punk rock chick."

"Oh yeah, well, I guess," I said dumbly. Whatever that meant. I looked at him. He was no prize himself. Pushing fifty. Built like a bear. Hair already white. I thought then of one of his books, wherein he waxed poetic about the sight of a woman slipping out of her panties. I realized I was wearing dull and ugly underwear.

"Come here," Andrew said. He grabbed my pinkie and pulled me toward him. He put his hands on my hips. This felt good. I leaned over and applied my lips to his. This was also good. Right then, as I swooned into this, my first kiss since Robbie the Teenage Alcoholic, a searchlight was trained upon us and a voice boomed out, "POLICE, EVERYBODY FREEZE."

Most of the poets were out cold anyway. This left me and Andrew to freeze. The cops came over then and told us we were camping illegally. They went around prodding all the prone bodies. When they were sure we were all on our feet and appeared to be getting ready to pile back in the van, they drove off, to go terrorize other illegal campers. Scotty was not even close to sober. Neither was Peter. And none of the rest of us knew how to drive. After all, poets don't drive. So we all lay down and went back to sleep. Whatever magic had been on the verge of weaving itself around Andrew and me was now gone. I slept next to Beth, with my head on her jacket.

In the morning we drove back to town and went our separate ways.

Over the next few months, Beth and I became close friends. We laughed at and gossiped about all the poets. The poets were all fucking one another and writing poems about it. Beth and I did not fuck each other. There was a moment when I think we both thought about it. But only fleetingly.

Heddy and Leah and Fran and I did not fuck one another. That is, Fran was out of the loop. Leah and Heddy and I, on the other hand, basically *did* fuck one another. One night I went with Heddy and Leah to a rock concert in Denver. At the end of the concert, as we were getting ready to leave, we spotted a really cute crew guy. Heddy and I simply commented on how cute he was, but Leah, newly single and very horny, wanted to do something about how cute he was. And so we ended up bringing this baffled and delighted British crew guy back to Boulder. In the end, it was really Heddy who had picked him up. Leah had gone coy at the moment of truth. And so Heddy had flexed her tattoos, swished her wide hips, and said, "How 'bout a ride to Boulder, young man." And now Heddy was going to take the guy home. But Leah wanted in on the fun. I did, too. Leah and I wouldn't take Heddy's hints when we were all four gathered at her house and she was suggesting it was time for me and Leah to leave. Instead, Leah took off her shirt. This was not out of character. Yuppies get horny, too. And because they often have the attitude that nothing can be denied them, they are good at getting their needs met. Leah was going to get her needs met. And she had nice tits. So she showed them. Crew Guy and Heddy and I were all sort of surprised at Leah standing there with her tits hanging out. Then we all started fucking one another.

Leah's tits broke the ice and pretty soon Crew Guy had his sizable dick inside of Heddy and his mouth on me and Leah was humping my leg while fondling herself. Just like that. One minute we were standing around awkwardly, the next we were bonking one another. At one point, I caught a slightly disturbed look on Heddy's face. Heddy had formerly been a prostitute. This was in her past. Now she was trying really hard to be an upstanding self-help book writer. She was trying to meet nice normal boys and not do it on the first date. I could see on her face that fucking some crew guy and two girls she usually had only clothed encounters with was kicking up her "issues." As for me, I was vaguely turned on but also off. I had had sex with girls twice in my life and both times they had been very thin, dainty junkie girls and it was strictly one on one, not an orgy situation. Now, more than a year after my last shot of dope, I was bonking two fat-assed sober chicks and a slightly smarmy English guy who lifted amplifiers for a living. Of the four of us, Leah was definitely getting the most out of this. I'll never forget this image of her: spread-eagle on the carpet, grinning madly while playing with herself with one hand, rubbing my tits with the other, and watching Heddy climb on top of Crew Guy and rock heartily back and forth on his big stiff dick. Leah was in heaven.

Leah must have had twenty-five orgasms while Heddy and Crew Guy and I made do with two apiece. I think at one point we all slept for a while. Around nine A.M. we got up, took turns in the shower, then all had coffee together. Only Leah seemed at ease. The rest of us couldn't look at one another. We were just uptight people sitting around drinking coffee and pretending we hadn't fucked one another all night. Eventually, Heddy drove Crew Guy back to his crew in Denver and Leah dropped me off at home.

By now I had moved out of my mother's basement and had a lit-tle two-bedroom house that I shared with Beth. When I walked in that morning, Beth asked where I'd been all night.

"Well, I was fucking my friends Leah and Heddy and some cute but smarmy English guy we picked up in Denver."

Beth laughed. "I really love your sense of humor," she said, then turned back to studying her massage therapy books.

About a month after Leah and Heddy and I fucked one another, Heddy decided to marry her boyfriend, who beat her up. This was a boyfriend she'd had on and off since her hooker days. At one point he'd been her pimp. He beat her repeatedly and she'd left him repeatedly. Now she had gone back to him and was going to marry him. It's often the toughest girls in the world who get beat by their boyfriends. I don't know why.

After Heddy married Bill, Leah and Fran and I stopped hearing from her. Leah was deeply absorbed in her capitalism courses at the university. Plus, she had to intern at some sort of hideous financial management plant. This brought on a whole new slew of outfits: taupes and mauves and flesh-colored stockings. And not much time for me or Fran. Fran, who was getting in deeper with her fat-assed girlfriend, was also going to marriage counseling with her husband. I had been taking on more hours at the café, since my beloved boss, Will, to my great chagrin, decided to move his family to a remote part of Montana and live off the land. I was promoted and given new shifts. These, combined with time spent hanging around the poets, took up most of my life. The Old Sluts Club was breaking up, and pretty soon Beth went zooming out of my life, too.

She had started holing up with Kendrick in his tiny apartment overlooking the gas station where he worked. They had been circling around each other for months, then one night she went home with him, they did the deed, and Beth basically moved in. Kendrick was waiting to hear whether he'd gotten a job teaching poetry at UCLA. The combined anxiety of working at a gas station and waiting to hear about the job made him do a lot of downers. Beth was afraid that if she left him alone he would die. And she loved him hopelessly. For nearly a month, she did not come home to our humble abode. Then one day she finally appeared. She looked haggard and tinier than usual, as if Kendrick, in all his psychotic convolutions, had sucked everything out of her.

"What happened?" I asked Beth as she stood listlessly in the middle of the living room.

"Oh . . ." she sighed, then let herself collapse onto the couch. "Kendrick went on a tirade last night. He didn't get the job at UCLA. So we went to hear some jazz in Denver. He got drunk. Took Vicodins. He flirted with a waitress and broke bottles. By the time we got home, he was totally nuts. I couldn't deal with him, so I took a Vicodin and passed out. When I came to, he was holding a knife to my throat. He said if I stopped loving him he'd kill me."

"Oh," I said. This kind of thing was too rich and overwrought for my blood. I had lately been holing up with a sweet but not terribly bright Buddhist percussionist named Timmy. Timmy was a sort of precursor to The Reader in that Timmy was my first foray into cute simple boys who don't really torture you. Timmy and I laughed and had sex and ate cherries in bed. We certainly did not hold knives to each other's throat while on a downers binge. Actually, it was incongruous that Beth, who I'd always taken to be a model for a certain breed of sanity, was now involved in a dramatic and psychotic relationship. But we all fall down the derisive devil hole of ill-placed obsession sometime. And this was Beth's time. She was, she told me in the next breath, moving with Kendrick to Hawaii, where Kendrick had decided he had to go to learn to surf while he completed a book of poems he was working on. Beth and Kendrick were going to pool together their modest financial resources and fly out there.

A few days later, Beth had packed up her belongings and I stood on the porch of our little house, bidding her adieu while she waited for Kendrick.

"I'm sorry, it was fun being roommates. I don't know why I'm leaving, but I have to," she said.

"Yeah," I said dejectedly, "that's how it goes." But I was mad. She was my friend and she was leaving our happy little house to go be nuts with a poet on downers. I resented her terribly.

That night, as Timmy and I lay in bed tickling each other and eating cherries, I decided it was time to move back to New York. I'd had enough fresh air and hippies and Buddhists. I'd finally written a second fuck book, which hopefully I'd sell. And Martin and Jane had offered me their couch for two weeks if I wanted to come back.

Leah drove me to the airport. She was wearing a pinstriped power suit, navy pumps, and hair pulled back in a tight bun. I was wearing ill-fitting pants, a tank top, sneakers, and a mop of multicolored hair. We must have looked like an odd pair as we walked through the airport.

"I guess this is the end of the Old Sluts Club," Leah said as we stood near my boarding gate. She said this with a tweaked little smile that remembered us bonking each other a mere six months earlier.

"No, we'll always be the Old Sluts."

"Yeah. I guess so," she said. She seemed very forlorn, as if this moment signified the end of her youth. Now she would forever be a grown-up. She'd have a career. She would get married, have kids, a house, a dog. No more bonking crew guys. Maybe she would get a weird flat accent. The way my old friend Hope had. For Hope's accent, once she'd married Pete the Truck Driver and started having kids, had gotten downright nasal. She was by now pregnant with the third kid, and when we had talked on the phone a few weeks earlier, the twang had been much more pronounced. It almost seemed as if the pregnancies, in distending her belly, had distended her voice box as well.

Maybe Leah would also acquire an accent. Or, more likely, she would be a power mother, sticking her kids in Ivy League Prep Kindergarten. And I would forage through the exterior world, searching and digging, burning and blumbering. There were no power careers or pregnancies in my immediate future, of that I was certain. Leah and I hugged each other and I boarded the plane. I watched Colorado get smaller as the jet soared up into pillowy clouds.

I moved onto Martin and Jane's couch and from there into a tiny furnished room in a single-occupancy hotel. The other residents were mostly bum-type guys with gin blossom noses and consumptive coughs.

My fuck book writing career was mottled. I couldn't always sell the books, and when I did, I had to wait forever for checks. I tried having an office job, but wearing office outfits depressed me too much. I became a bottle-picker-upper at a nightclub and, ultimately, a receptionist at the dungeon.

One day I was out shopping for cleaning products for the dominatrixes to give their johns—demeaned-through-cleaning fantasies were a specialty of the house. I was in the supermarket's cleaning products aisle, and as I reached to the uppermost shelf for some bathroom cleaner, I knocked a jug over and it bonked an innocent bystander on the head. There was an audible *twonk,* and my victim looked at me bafflingly, thinking, apparently, that I had twonked him on purpose. I apologized. I offered to buy him a cup of coffee. He was shy and gentle. A few weeks later, we went to his grandparents' cabin upstate. On the train I ate too many apricots and then oozed sulfuric stench all weekend. Then, a few months later, in spite of the fact that he had ignored my sulfuric shit smell, I moved in with him. And then out.

I then moved to Sixth Street. I pole-vaulted Dave With the Long Dick. After Dave came Edgar, who taught me to say "motherfucker" right. It was around this time that Beth came to visit me in New York for the first time. After two years, she had finally left Kendrick, who, in the end, had holed up in their little shack in Maui, refusing to go outside. Refusing to let Beth go outside. Kendrick had snapped. Finally, his parents had come for him and a thoroughly depleted Beth had moved onto her childhood friend Mary's couch in Milwaukee.

Not long after that, I was in Milwaukee with my dominatrix boss, who was on a book tour promoting her tawdry tome *The Politically Correct Dominatrix.* We were traveling in style. I had my own suite in a swank and modern hotel. Beth came to visit me there.

"Isn't this great?" I said, motioning to my swank surroundings. "Look, look at all the stuff." I opened the mini-fridge for her. Inside it were diminutive bottles of booze and overpriced mass-produced gourmet goods. "Want some five-dollar water?"

Beth barely cracked a smile. She sat down on the plush couch and for the next forty-five minutes did not move. She was different. Kendrick had taken something out of her and she had let him. And I wasn't at my most attentive. I had that afternoon met a cute young poet in a bookstore. I had him scheduled in right after Beth. When I told her that I had a boy coming over in a mere half hour, her lips drew tightly together, she pressed her palms against her knees in a weird tense gesture I'd never seen before, and she said, "Well, I don't want to keep you."

"Hey no, wait no, don't go, I didn't mean to chase you out or anything, you can stay, we can all hang out together." I think she almost spat on me at that point. She left a few minutes later. I felt guilty. But then, Max the Poet came to visit and I ceased to muse upon my friend's broken soul.

I had apparently scared Max the Poet when I'd tried to pick him up in the bookstore, for now he brought a chaperone with him. The chaperone was a guy named Seth, who looked like a farmer on acid. Seth was also a poet. He and Max, in fact, often wrote together. They also talked together, completing each other's sentences, like a long-married couple. For a moment I wondered if they were in fact bonking each other. Then Seth began rhapsodising about a girl he'd met a week earlier. They were a weird pair. But I found Max's strange psychic link to his friend endearing, and when they proposed that we all three go out for a scenic tour of Milwaukee, I agreed.

We headed down a narrow side street. A bum was walking ahead of us. He had a bad limp and a paper bag pulled over part of his face.

"That guy," Seth said, motioning to the bum, "turns out that guy does great work."

"Oh yeah," Max said, "turns out that's why he wears a bag on his head. That guy's not a complete crazy man, he's a genius. He's seen the best minds of his generation wearing paper bags on their heads. That's the kind of guy he is."

A few blocks later, we passed a green-haired girl carrying a stepladder. Seth said, "Turns out that girl's the love of my life, but she's a voyeur and she takes her stepladder around and peeps into people's windows while thinking about *me* and this is how she gets off and I understand her pain but we are like ships in the night."

When I asked Max if he wanted to come back to my room, sans chaperone, he looked very nervous.

"Oh, I don't know about all that. I mean, if I came up with you, well, then, *things* might happen, and turns out I don't know if I'm up for things happening."

I pressed a little further. And got nowhere. They walked me back to the hotel lobby, but when I tried to kiss Max, he backed away, shaking his head: "Oh no, no, I can't do things like that."

I rolled my eyes and shrugged. "Well, write me a letter or something, then." I went back to my plush room, put Max out of my mind, tried to call Beth, who was not at home, then fell asleep and, the next day, continued on with Belle the Dominatrix and her whirlwind mini-tour.

When I got back to New York, there was indeed a letter from Max.

Dear Zoe:
The other day
I was sitting here thinking of you
I was really confused about you
So I took a shower and made a sandwich
But then when I was done with all that
I was still really confused
You see sometimes when you're writing a poem
And you just can't seem to get it
You go over and you make a sandwich and you come back
     and you've got it
And it's almost like the sandwich taught you how to write
     the poem
But somehow that stuff doesn't work with you.
Love,
Max

This letter was followed by another, and soon Max was outright courting me via the U.S. mail. Meanwhile, as Max penned love letters from Milwaukee, Beth, who did not know Max, moved off her friend Mary's couch and into her own apartment, which was a few streets away from where Max lived.

A few weeks later, Max decided to move to New York to seek his poetry fortune and, I suppose, woo me.

Dear Zoe:
I will arrive in two weeks.
I will live in my mom's living room until I find a job.
I am moving up in the world
From my dad's basement in Idaho
To my mother's living room in New York.
Actually I should come clean with you.
I never really lived in my dad's basement.
I had a real room
Ground level but
My poetry agent told me to tell everyone that I lived in
    my dad's basement as a way to milk this whole
    "slacker" thing.
Love,
Max

Max, who didn't believe in airplanes, arrived by train. He came right from Penn Station to my house. He had two duffel bags. He sat them down on my floor and we kissed. The kiss was a good kiss and it turned into *things* and *things* turned into more *things* and a few weeks passed. Max settled into his mom's living room and got a bike messenger job.

Max became one of those dangerous jerks on a bike, zipping blindly through traffic, pedaling faster than hell itself to deliver things to people. At the end of the day, he'd come over, tired, with his thighs bulging from biking.

Sometimes we went out to movies or poetry readings. Other times we'd hole up and watch movies at home. We were so happy.

One night Max and I were lying naked in bed. Max said, "I'm hungry for pancakes. I would like to go to the all-night diner. We'll have that 'just got fucked' look on our faces. We will sit eating pancakes and looking well-fucked."

We put on clothes and went to the all-night diner, where we ate pancakes. The waiter, a tall, skinny Polish guy who always flirts with me, was visibly upset. He could see the "just got fucked" look on my face. He wished he had put it there.

Max and I were starting to run out of things to talk about. This had been happening for a week or so. Max had now been in New York for a month, and although we were enmeshed, we didn't have that much to say to each other.

Max put a forkful of pancakes in his mouth. Then he gestured toward the Polish waiter who wished he'd put the "just got fucked" look on my face, and said, "Turns out that guy does really good work."

"Yeah," I said halfheartedly. The phrase "Turns out" was wearing thin and I couldn't find what if anything was beneath it.

We walked back to Sixth Street. We were coming into my building when a dark-clad figure rushed in behind us and narrowly tailed us up the stairs, breathing heavily and reeking of something weird. I knew this was my neighbor, probably on a speed binge, hence the bulging eyes and jerky body motions. Max did not know this. Max thought the guy was a complete crazy man out to kill us.

As we reached the narrow corridor leading to both my and my neighbor's apartments, Max scurried ahead, putting *me* between himself and my speedy neighbor. I opened the apartment door and Max barreled in as my neighbor fidgeted with his own lock.

"God, Max, why'd you rush in like that? You practically knocked me over."

"That Eye Guy, what was that Eye Guy doing? He was gonna mug us?"

"That's my *neighbor*. He *lives* there. He wasn't trying to *mug* us, he's just a speed freak. God, and what, you put *me* between you and the guy you thought was gonna put an ice pick in us? What the fuck kind of chivalry is *that*?"

Max just shrugged. Max was twenty-two, and I, at that point, was twenty-seven. I was at the tail end of a generation of girls who wanted a guy to take an ice pick in the ribs for them. Max was of a generation that believes in self-preservation at all costs. Even if the cost is that the person you're sleeping with gets ice-picked. This was what made me know I couldn't love Max. He would let me get ice-picked in the ribs.

A few nights later, Max came over and said, "Turns out this just isn't working out so well, huh?"

"Yes," I said, "turns out I think you're right."

Ours was to be an amicable parting. We stood hugging. Max patted me on the back. I had, this back-patting implied, already been demoted from girlfriend to pal. He patted a while longer, then left. A few weeks later, he called to say he was going back to Milwaukee. I told him to look Beth up if he ever needed a massage. Of course, I hadn't talked to Beth in a long time. But I assumed she'd be happy to earn some bucks rubbing Max's back.

And then, long after Max had gone, Eye Guy remained Eye Guy. Whenever I heard his speed metal records throbbing through the walls, I thought, Ah, Eye Guy is having a good time with his speed metal. I developed a sort of fondness for Eye Guy. I felt for him the tenderness you have for a stranger whose humanity you have heard shrieking through the walls.

One day, Eye Guy found love. Eye Girl moved in. I didn't actually see Eye Girl move in. I became aware that a girl had moved in with Eye Guy because I started to hear them fight. I'd hear them fight and then fuck. Loudly. Eye Girl was a screamer. The way Eye Girl screamed, you could feel the claw marks on Eye Guy's back as she ripped his flesh during sex. She screamed so hard you could imagine her face twisting up ballistically as she frantically searched through her huge trunk full of sex toys, seeking out enormous vibrating steel things that she strapped on and brandished at Eye Guy, Eye Guy lying back almost bashfully, his Eye Guy eyes barely bulging at all as Eye Girl, I imagined, made him put on a leather clown suit. I imagined her holding a knife to his throat: "DO IT, EYE GUY, DO IT, PUT ON THE LEATHER OUTFIT, EYE GUY, PUT IT ON NOW OR DIE, EYE GUY, DIE, EYE GUY, DIE."

Of course, she probably didn't call him Eye Guy.

One day, a few months after Max went home to Milwaukee, I went up and knocked on the door of my upstairs neighbor Oliver the Bassoon Player. I had met him one day when I'd lost my house keys. He had let me climb through his window and down the fire escape into my own apartment. As I was climbing out his window, he tried to pick me up. But, at the time, I was in the throes of Max. Now, however, I was in the throes of nothing and no one. And so I knocked on Oliver's door. Oliver was a beautiful bassoon player. He was also a former crack addict. This he told me as we walked over to Theater 80, where we were going to see *Play Misty for Me.*

"Yeah," Oliver said with a little smile, "I scraped shit off the bottom of hell's shoe. For two months I lived out of a shopping cart. I was one of those guys that goes around collecting crap out of Dumpsters, then selling it on Second Avenue. At night I slept on the subway. I'm all better now, though," he said brightly. "That was more than five years ago."

Oliver and I held hands as we watched Clint Eastwood play a late-night dejay who is stalked and nearly killed by a demented girl who keeps requesting the song "Misty." She keeps calling him up and, in varying shades of sinister, requesting the song. Ultimately she nearly offs poor Clint Eastwood. But not quite. Clint wins. Of course.

"That's some movie," I said as we left the theater. "You ever get stalked?"

"Oh yeah, a lot actually."

"A lot? Why?"

"I used to play in a band called Piss Horse. We'd start riots and burn stuff. Mostly people hated us, but when they liked us, they REALLY liked us."

"You played bassoon in Piss Horse?"

"Drums."

"Oh."

"Drumming attracts a certain element. It's more primal than bassoon. There was one girl in particular who went nuts for me. She was sort of cute, kind of like this Upper East Side girl gone bad. She looked very uptown except she had these incredibly long fingernails. Like out to here," he said, holding his hand out a good eight inches. "Gnarly fingernails. But kind of a turn-on. So I slept with her a couple of times but we just didn't click, so well, so then I tried to end it and she went ape shit. She started calling all the time and leaving shit at my doorstep. She would like cut off pieces of her fingernails and stick them in the eyes of a doll and then smear blood all over it and leave it on my doorstep. It got scary."

"That's endearing. Jesus. Then what'd you do?"

"Well, then one night I ran into her at a club. I saw her a few feet away, so I bolted in the other direction and she followed. She followed me all the way out to the alley behind the club and had me pinned against a wall. Then she started yelling all this shit at me and trying to POKE me with her fingernails."

"Ugh."

"Yeah, but then this guy *Bubba*, who's in some weird German industrial band and plays like chain saw or something, he suddenly appears in the alley and the girl just totally forgets about me, she walks up to Bubba and starts talking to him. Next thing I hear, she's like living with Bubba in a condo in Rotterdam."

Oliver was very lighthearted about the many mishaps and poisoned adventures he'd lived through. And that was sexy. We shacked up for three weeks. He tied me up. I raked my burred fingernails down his back. We enjoyed each other's company, but there was fear breeding between us. Oliver and I were from the same mold and this, I think, made us squeamish. One day Oliver decided to go hitchhiking through Ecuador. When he came back, I had met and fallen in love with Bev. Oliver moved out of the building shortly after that. This had nothing to do with my taking up with Bev. Oliver was simply sick of living above Eye Guy. Eye Guy and Eye Girl were too loud.

A few months after this, Oliver and I began to forge a sturdy and sexy friendship. This involved going to movies and holding hands. It involved calling each other almost daily. It never involved getting naked. For that I had Bev and then Satan. Oliver had a succession of women and then Bonnie the Brilliant Nympho. Sometimes Oliver and I would have long dinners with his friend Merle the Former Dope Fiend and my friend Jane. We all four had been spat through detoxes and rehabs and self-help programs. We took to calling ourselves Idiots Anonymous and swapping stories.

One day, not so long ago, I brought Beth with me to an Idiots Anonymous dinner. She and I had, over time, grown close again. Now she'd come for a visit. This was after I had left Bev for Satan. This was after Satan had left me but before I came to hold a vigil in his closet with a bike chain in my lap.

The Idiots were meeting at Mogador. In fact, the very same waitress who was once in Bev's rock video and once waited on Jane and me when Dave With the Long Dick sat nearby, this same waitress waited on the Idiots. Beth, I could see, felt slightly uncomfortable. Particularly when Tina, who had suddenly ballooned up by a good twenty pounds, expounded upon a recent binge: "I just couldn't stop. Day in and day out for the last seventeen days. I ate and ate and puked and ate. Then I began taking enormous doses of Ex-Lax so I'd evacuate my fat. But it didn't work. I just made a mess of my bathroom. And look at me, I'm fat, I'm completely fat."

"Tina, if you're fat, then what am I?" asked Merle, who actually WAS fat. Tina looked uncomfortable. Tina, who was, after all, a terribly well-bred bulimic, tried to counter this with grace.

"You're uh . . . portly, Merle, but you're a man. Men get laid no matter what their appearance. What would be perceived as grotesque in a woman might be found endearing in a man."

"Tina, I'd sleep with you even if you weighed five hundred pounds and could not leave the house," Oliver offered then. The thought of weighing five hundred pounds so horrified Tina that she had to leave the table. I pinched Oliver's forearm. "You didn't have to freak her out like that," I said. Oliver smiled his most puckish smile.

Beth, at this point, was picking at her food halfheartedly. I thought she'd jump right in and tell us all about the succession of psychopath boyfriends she'd had since Kendrick. For Kendrick had apparently opened a "psychopath wanted" door in Beth. Where she had always been one to veer toward gentle souls, since Kendrick, her stability sensors had gone haywire. Both, however, did not volunteer for us any details of Lurid Love. She didn't seem to understand our need to blather at one another about our excesses. She sat brooding slightly as Jane recounted her near decade living on chocolate and methadone, lying in bed, reading Balzac and Márquez over and over and over. Beth did not even look interested when David the Sex Addict told us about his weekend with a transvestite hooker on acid.

"You really hated that, didn't you?" I asked Beth as we headed home to my hovel.

"Oh, not at all. I think it's tender."

"Tender?"

"Yes. Tender. But it's not for me."

"Oh."

We went back to my apartment. Eye Guy's speed metal was screaming through the walls. He was really hitting it hard now. A few days earlier, after a particularly voluble battle, Eye Girl had left Eye Guy. And now, as Beth and I sat talking, listening to records and evaluating our lives, Eye Guy speed-metaled his heartbreak away. Beth and I put on a Górecki CD to drown out the speed metal. We each lit a cigarette and sat on the couch, listening.

"There's something I didn't tell you," Beth said, stubbing out a Marlboro and opening her eyes to their widest and most earnest setting.

I arched my brows. "Yeah?"

"Max."

"Max?"

"I've fallen in love with Max."

"Who's Max?"

"Max, the poet. Max, the one *you* were in love with."

"No , *really*?"

"Do you hate me now?"

"Hate you?"

"You're not angry?"

"Why would I be?"

"We've never shared a guy before."

"We're hardly SHARING him. I mean, that was two years ago and it didn't work out at all. He would have let me get ice-picked in the ribs."

"What?"

I told her about the night when Max rushed in my apartment, putting me between himself and what he perceived to be a very dangerous Eye Guy. I told her how this turned my heart cold and final. She got a dreamy look on her face. "Oh, he's such a child," she said fondly.

"But you really like him?"

"He makes my heart boom."

"And you're happy?"

"So far. Yes. I am."

After a while, she admitted she'd gone so far as to let Max the Poet move in with her. He had gotten a janitor job and was working on a first novel. And living with her. And this, she said, made her happy. But there were complications. There was the complication that Max is puppy-dog outgoing while Beth is reclusive. There is the generational difference. Max is ten years younger than Beth. There is the mortal combat of two souls struggling for a place to call their own.

Beth and I had lost that place but now found it again. We fell apart, then came back together.

Later that day, as we were leaving the hovel, we saw Eye Girl come back. She had put pink streaks in her hair. "Hi," I said as we passed in the hall.

"Yeah, yeah," she said, brushing by us and letting herself into her and Eye Guy's apartment.

"Oh, honey, you're home," we heard Eye Guy say.

Beth and I went and had Italian food, then shoe-shopped. We both found shoes. She found tiny size-five boots because she has tiny feet. I found big size-nine shoes because I have big feet. I am only five foot four, a hundred and fifteen pounds. There's no reason for such big feet.

The next day, I noticed a peculiar smell emanating from Eye Guy's door. And he and Eye Girl were disconcertingly quiet. Beth and I heard nothing at all. No couch throwing, no screams, no fucking.

A couple nights later, Jane came by to join and Beth and me and watching movies. We were getting toward the heartrending end of *Edward Scissorhands*, one of my very favorites, which I had forced the Buñuel- and Pasolini-inclined Beth and Jane to watch with me. As poor Edward abandoned love and returned to his castle, as my own eyes swelled, I heard a scratching noise coming from the hall. Jane and I looked at each other.

"What's that?" Jane said.

"I don't know. Maybe it's Eye Guy scratching at the door. He's been gone, you know. For three days I haven't heard a peep out of those two." Jane, of course, knew all about Eye Guy and my fascination with him. Jane was the only person on earth, save Max the Poet, who understood my fascination with Eye Guy. Bev, although he had humored me, had never really understood why I liked to eavesdrop on Eye Guy. Satan didn't understand either. Beth, although she was trying and although she was in fact fucking the guy who had named Eye Guy, did not really get it either.

Jane and I tiptoed over to the peephole. I looked through and saw Daisy the Stripper yanking on the leash of her Doberman, Pokey. Pokey was FURIOUSLY scratching at Eye Guy and Eye Girl's door. As if he were smelling dinner. And Daisy was yanking on Pokey, trying to get him away from the door. I watched for several minutes until finally Daisy pulled the dog away.

"That was Daisy the Stripper," I told Jane.

"Yeah? Why was her dog scratching at Eye Guy's door?"

"Maybe Eye Girl killed Eye Guy and she's got pieces of his body hanging around the apartment, attracting flies. The dog smelled dinner." Jane giggled at this. The possibility of my next-door neighbor's body decomposing there, a mere few feet away from where we were standing—this possibility was as fascinating as Dave's long dick. Jane even said, "Eye Guy is proving to be more interesting than the guy with the long dick." Then we had to explain it to Beth. We had to show her how long the long dick was. Practically as long as my torso. Beth was intrigued. Beth was much more interested in the long dick than in the possibility of Eye Guy's body decomposing. The next morning, as Beth packed up and prepared to go home to Milwaukee, she said that if things didn't work out with Max, she wanted to meet the guy with the long dick. "Oh yeah, well, he's married now, though," I told her.

"Oh," she said. I think that she had, for a moment, had big plans for the guy with the long dick. "It's just as well. I'm happy with Max," she said. We kissed each other's cheek and hugged. Beth went home to Milwaukee.

A few days later, I heard Daisy and her dog at Eye Guy's door again. Scratching. I opened my own door and confronted Daisy.

"Daisy, what's up with your dog?" I said.

"What?" She wheeled around.

"Why's your dog keep scratching at Eye Guy's door?"

"What do you mean? Who's Eye Guy?"

"Eye Guy, the guy that lives in there with the blond girl," I said, motioning to Eye Guy's door.

"Oh, you mean Frank?" Daisy said. "His name is Frank. He disappeared a few days ago. Didn't you know?"

"No, what do you mean, disappeared? Where'd he go?"

"No one knows. Linda's heartbroken."

"Who's Linda?"

"Your neighbor, Zoe, the blonde. She's pretty worked up about the whole thing. She doesn't have any way to pay the rent 'cause Frank was supporting her and he didn't pay this month's rent, so Linda, she's on this thing where she goes in Key Food and steals MEAT. You wouldn't believe it, but you can actually go into some of the neighborhood bodegas and sell steaks and shit and get pretty good bucks for it. So she's always coming in with STEAKS in her pockets and THAT's what my dog smells, he smells a STEAK TRAIL."

"Get outta here, really?"

"Sure." Daisy shrugged, yanked on her dog's leash, gave me a funny look, then walked away. When she got downstairs to the first floor, I heard her knock on Lonette's door: "Girl, I'm going to the store, you need anything?"

"Yeah, I need a man, Daisy, you got one of those for me?"

I heard Daisy laugh.

As for Eye Guy, I guess I'll never know what happened to him. He never came back. Hopefully, wherever he went, he's better off. Maybe he's sitting in some swank penthouse, being kept by a loony rich lady who likes to bondage him up and torture his poor Eye Guy dick. Maybe he got carted away to Bellevue and is in a ward near Billie May, who shot the Heavy Metal Guitarist in the leg. Or maybe he's in detox and will soon be joined by the Hefty Lesbian at the end of her current crack run. Or maybe Eye Guy moved to the suburbs. Maybe Eye Guy lives in a trailer now. No more speed metal, my Eye Guy's working in a box factory in Jersey, and he couldn't be happier.

I don't know. I don't know where Eye Guy went, but I wish him the best, I really do.

17

I Want Candy

I wish Beth were here. Where I sit now. In the closet. I wish Beth were here to help me tie Satan up and make him mop. But she is not. I have, out of boredom, started foraging through Satan's drawers again, unearthing things that invoke shotgun blasts of memory. Satan, for some reason, still has the airline ticket stub from our Florida trip. Perhaps to commemorate those last few days before we broke up. Satan, with his inimitable timing, broke up with me a week after my father died unexpectedly.

Charlie was not yet sixty. He'd been suffering side effects of the multitudinous bones and organs he'd broken and pierced while training horses. This, along with brutally high blood pressure and various smoker's diseases, had conspired to kill him. I don't think he knew it was coming. I certainly didn't. By now we had grown close again. We spoke on the phone weekly and fondly. We were friends. And then his heart just quit working in the middle of the night. He died in an emergency room in Florida, where he was living. A nurse called me at five A.M. "Your father has passed away." Pause. "What shall we do with, er . . . the *body?*" she said with the required faux-reverent tone. My limbs went numb and the whole floating earth stopped twirling.

"Er . . . Are you there, miss?" came the nurse's voice.

"I'll have to call you back," I said then. I hung up. I looked at the ceiling, as if its cracks would let in crevices of some weird heaven where perhaps Charlie was floating. I started to sob then, sobbing from deep down. From a place I didn't know existed.

Satan came with me to Florida the next day. Satan and I had been together nearly a year by now. We were walking the serrated edges of intimacy. They were slicing into our feet. Blood was spurting out in awkward jets, and then, just when it appeared I would bleed to death, the coagulant of tenderness filled in the wounds. Which is to say, I was out on an uncomfortable limb, staying with Satan long after Repulsion had gallivanted in the door and performed a hideous jig of flailing arms and flying fluids. Yet every time I thought of bolting, Satan somehow held my interest. And now Satan was coming with me to Florida, to go tend to Charlie's affairs.

Charlie's death had caused his old cronies to surface. Through their peculiar horse people grapevine, they all got wind of it. Nicholas had his fifth wife call to tell me that Nicholas, whom I hadn't seen since age sixteen, would come to Florida to help me sort things out. Molly called. She and I hadn't spoken in ages. She was now crippled and in a wheelchair. Five years earlier, her boyfriend had gotten mad at her. As she stood up to walk out of their apartment, he shot her in the back with a deer-hunting rifle. She was in the hospital for six months and emerged paralyzed from the waist down. Now she negotiated life from a wheelchair. She called and said that she, too, would meet me in Florida.

Satan and I flew down and took a room at a Holiday Inn on a freeway near the funeral parlor. Molly, driving a handicapped-friendly car, picked us up at the airport. We deplaned and there she was. Waiting at the gate in a high-tech wheelchair. Her face was a mixture of sadness and radiance. I leaned down and hugged her. I felt her tears on my cheek. We held each other for a few moments, then I introduced her to Satan. She shook Satan's hand.

"Damn, Zoe, you didn't tell me your boyfriend was beautiful," she said. I saw Satan wince at the compliment. Then paste on a smile that he offered to Molly.

We tooled through the airport and out to Molly's car. Satan and I helped her get from the chair into the car. This involved wedging our hands under her butt. She made salacious cracks as we did this. Then, as she turned the key in the ignition, her mood changed and tears came again. I wrapped my arms around her. "I can't believe he's gone," she said through sobs.

We drove to the funeral parlor. It was hot and I was numb. The funeral director, one Mr. Bryant, a smarmy, smooth-toned individual with slicked-back hair and a drawl, sneered when I picked out a simple cardboard box for Charlie's ashes. Smarmy Bryant had shown me various hideous high-priced urns. Although I didn't know exactly what Charlie would want, I did not think a hideous urn would be it. I even called my mother in the middle of these urn negotiations. "Do you know what my dad would want done with his body?" I asked Francine. Francine, I could hear through the phone wires, was nearly choking. She wanted to say something warm about the man she had once been married to. She wanted to offer me comfort. But she didn't know how. All she said was, "Zoe, I just don't know."

I chose the economical cardboard box and signed papers. Papers that said it was all right to burn my father's body and put the remains in a box. Smarmy said it would take a few days to perform the task of burning Charlie's body. He would, he said, MAIL me the ashes. When I questioned the reliability of such a thing, he said, "We've had very few people get lost in the mail."

When Molly and Satan and I got back into the car, Molly started cracking wise about Charlie: "It'd be just like that old dog to get lost in the mail. End up at some cute redhead's P.O. box." She laughed. Then she cried. She put the car in drive and we went to Charlie's apartment.

Charlie had been renting a tiny apartment from one of the multitudinous Horse Ladies he knew. Horse Ladies are women pushing forty who seldom get laid and relate to animals more than people. They invariably own large dogs and cheap modern furniture. They have well-developed biceps. They are often blond. They are weatherbeaten. They always loved Charlie. They rented him apartments at below market value. They took care of him a little, and eventually, when Charlie didn't put out, they got mad at him.

After a five-year streak of ill health and crappy jobs, Charlie's luck had just been starting to change. He'd been feeling better. He'd been taking fewer medications. He'd been starting to give riding lessons again and orchestrating horse sales. He'd even been dating a girl after a long dry spell. Then Zazu, a Horse Lady Charlie had sold a horse to fairly recently, had rented him this apartment, which adjoined her own.

As Satan and Molly and I entered Zazu's apartment, I could feel the resentment. She was mad as hell that Charlie had died. She had, in all likelihood, done a lot of caretaking. And Charlie, who had always expected people to want to take care of him, probably took her for granted. And then died. In the apartment she owned.

As Zazu's large dogs sniffed at all our crotches, she showed us into Charlie's tiny abode next door. Here, everything was tidy and Charlie-like. When I looked in the closet and saw his pants, dozens and dozens of them, neatly pressed and hanging, I wept. I sat down on the tiny floor of the closet and wept. Satan put his arm on my shoulder. Molly hung her head. Zazu retreated into her own apartment.

We spent several hours in there. It was bewildering that Charlie's stuff was there, reduced to a fraction of essentials, but that Charlie himself was gone.

"Your father really was a character," Satan said at one point, having unearthed a trunk full of cowboy boots, all in superb condition. There were red ones, green ones, blue ones, black ones. All very similar-looking.

"Yeah, he liked his stuff, that's for sure. He'd go on these sprees, whenever he got some money, just go out and buy six pairs of boots or three suede jackets. Whenever he found something he liked, he bought as many variations of it as he could find."

Satan tried on one of Charlie's suede jackets. This made me twitch slightly. All the same, I offered it to him. "You can have it. Looks good on you." Satan regarded himself in the mirror. I wondered if Charlie was watching, if he was in some Bardo, glancing down, seeing Satan in his suede and shaking his head. "Zoe, what's the devil doing in my jacket?" he'd have said. Or maybe he would have liked Satan. I didn't know.

In the bottom drawer of Charlie's dresser I found a suitcase full of empty plastic containers. He had always loved anything that would hold stuff and had had more containers than stuff to put in them. This love of containers had apparently evolved into a veritable mania. There were dozens of containers of varying sizes. In the closet, I found nearly thirty suitcases. All empty. All of them cheap but in perfect upkeep. It was as if he had been striving to contain everything and that, had he lived a longer life, he would have had an entire apartment full of empty containers ready to be filled. Just in case he needed them one day. Just in case the gods showered upon him a great mound of STUFF. Charlie would have been ready.

It was nighttime when we finished going through Charlie's apartment. I'd collected any important-looking papers, some photographs, and a few pieces of clothing. The rest would go to the Salvation Army. There was nothing of value. Charlie had not left much behind. No money or property. Just a lot of containers and boots.

We were all exhausted by now. Molly, who was spending the night with an aunt who lived nearby, dropped Satan and me back at the Holiday Inn. Satan took his various medications and passed out. I lay awake, listening to the whir of the air conditioner. After a while, I pulled out a detective novel and read about people getting murdered. Sleep came at last.

The next day there was a sort of informal memorial service for Charlie. All the Florida Horse Ladies had gotten together and organized it. A skinny rich woman named Robin, who had, I learned, taken riding lessons from Charlie, had offered her house for the occasion. Nicholas, it was rumored, was going to appear there. Even here in Florida, Nicholas the Reformed Horse Thief was a legend. When Molly and Satan and I arrived at Robin's posh suburban spread, we were informed that Nicholas was on his way. I could tell from the way Robin said Nicholas's name that his charm was not lost on her.

Robin was a tall good-looking brunette pushing forty. She was dressed elegantly but wore too much jewelry and perfume. And there was something horribly needy in her eyes. This was another classic Horse Lady characteristic, one particularly prevalent in rich Horse Ladies. They *needed* but they didn't know exactly what they needed. They were searching. They were grasping at emptiness. And no amount of cash or horses could fill them. Not infrequently, they had thought Charlie could fill them. And he could. For a few weeks. I did not know whether or not Charlie had tried to fill Robin. But if he had, he hadn't succeeded. She looked at me probingly, searching my face for traces of Charlie, traces with which she could conduct unfinished business. "So you're Zoe," she said. "You look just like your father."

"Oh, uh, thanks."

"I'm very sorry about your loss."

"Thank you."

"You live in New York?"

"Yeah."

"And what do you do there?"

"Oh, uh, I write."

"Oh? For a magazine?"

"No, uh, books."

"Oh, well, isn't that wonderful! You know, Charlie never seemed to know what you did. Don't get me wrong, he loved you, he was proud of you, but he didn't know what you did. He said something to do with writing. But he didn't really know what. What kind of writing *do* you do?"

"Uh, sort of, uh, erotica."

"Oh." This frightened her into silence. She blinked at me, then twirled off to tend to some arriving guests. Satan and I sat down and watched people arrive. Some of them Charlie had known for years, most of them he had only met recently. A few faces were familiar from childhood, for, although we'd never lived in Florida, horse people all travel a certain circuit and, accordingly, some who were now here in Florida had been in Pennsylvania or Georgia or New York when I was a kid. They all said things to me and looked grave. Many of them looked at me expectantly. This confused me. I didn't know what they wanted. Was I supposed to utter reassuring bon mots? Was I supposed to look more heartbroken than I did? Less? I had never been at a funeral before. I had never, for that matter been at a wedding, a christening, or anything like this.

Just as I was feeling on the verge of really losing it Nicholas appeared. The small sea of people parted and there he was. I don't know how I'd expected him to look. Old, battered, fucked up. Instead, he looked the same. A little older, better dressed, but the same. "Zoe," he said, making my name into a profound statement of sorrow. He rested his hand in the small of my back and said, "I'm so sorry, darlin'." I said nothing. After a few long seconds Nicholas said, "You're more beautiful than ever," and twinkled his eyes at me. One minute he was my father's grief-stricken best friend, the next he was the first guy I fucked, possibly vying to be the next.

We stood like that for quite a while. I introduced him to Satan, who was standing at my side. Nicholas narrowed his eyes at Satan. Satan narrowed his eyes at Nicholas.

Nicholas held my hand and we walked over to where the guests were gathered. "You wanna say a few words?" he asked.

"No, I can't talk. I wouldn't know what to say. You say something."

Everyone was standing in a semicircle now. Robin and Nicholas and I stood in the middle. Robin said a few words. "I guess we're all gonna miss Charlie. I know I am. There's no one like him. He taught me a lot more than riding. He taught me about my own soul. And he made me mad as hell half the time. But I loved him." Everyone nodded solemnly. Then Nicholas cleared his throat and spoke.

"Well, just like ol' Charlie to leave us in a pinch here. I thought me and him'd be having adventures another twenty years or so. He was a beautiful human and there's always gonna be a Charlie-sized hole in my heart. I'd like to propose a toast: To Charlie, wherever you are, I know you found the cutest girl and the fanciest horse and, hell, have a good time." Nicholas raised his glass toward the sky. The others followed suit.

The gathering lightened then. Nicholas had suceeded in invoking the heartbreak, humor, and beauty of Charlie. And everyone felt better for it. As the evening wore on, Nicholas pulled a long succession of Charlie stories from his hat. There was the time the two of them got drunk, flew to Miami, rented a pink Cadillac, and cruised blondes. There was the five years they didn't speak to each other after Nicholas caught Charlie making out with his wife. Mostly, though, there was love. Satan was eyeballing Nicholas with fascination. He knew the story, he knew there was a tiny part of me that in some way would always belong inside Nicholas. And this, I think, bothered him. His eyes became speculative slits whenever they alighted upon Nicholas.

At the end of the night, Nicholas and I said our good-byes. He hugged me, placing his hand once more in the small of my back. "Darlin', I know your dad's gone now, but you got me. Anything you need. I don't care if you killed somebody, robbed a bank, or just want a shoulder to cry on, you can come to me." I smiled and nodded, even though there was a decent chance I would never speak to him again.

The next morning, Molly drove Satan and me to the airport. We sat for a few minutes in the passenger discharge loop while Molly and I exchanged phone numbers and addresses. Although there was love between us, I suspected I'd never see Molly again either. We lived in different worlds.

We hugged hard, putting tears on each other's cheeks. Then Satan and I flew home. As we sat in our little airplane seats, each lost in our own ruminations, I could feel that something strange was gathering in him. I did not know what it was, though.

I couldn't bear to go back to my hovel and so went with Satan to Eleventh Street. As he busied himself returning phone calls and instructing his assistant to grocery shop, pick up the cleaning, and schedule him a shrink appointment, I lurked around, lying about on the pricey but cruel red couch that was not only ugly but uncomfortable as well.

When Satan had temporarily finished orchestrating the next phase of his World Domination, he sat down at the other end of the couch and looked at me hard.

"You love everybody, don't you?" he said then.

"What?"

"You love Nicholas, don't you?"

"Well, sure I love him. I'm not in love with him, but I love him." What was he getting at? Did he really think the guy I fucked at fifteen was a threat? He couldn't possibly.

"And that friend of yours, that fucking psycho bassoon player you hang out with all the time. You love him, too."

"Well, yeah, he's my friend. Sure. I love him. What are you getting at?"

"You're just a glutton for love. I'm not enough for you. You have to have the whole world in love with you."

"What are you talking about?"

"You're like a happy puppy slapping along on its big paws, kissing everybody, trying to get everyone's attention. You're a goddamned pivot."

"I beg your pardon?"

"The Shah of Iran. Called himself the Pivot of the Universe. That's what you are. You're an emotional idiot pivot." It was a funny sentence but Satan was dead serious. Satan curled his lip at me to punctuate this statement. He might as well have sprayed me with bullets. He was gutting me. Out of the blue. Four days after my father had died.

"What on earth is up YOUR ass?" I said, trying to bristle but just feeling kicked.

"You're up my ass. Like a goddamned TAPEWORM. I try to stand by you. Your father dies, I go down and go through the whole thing with you. I didn't have to do that. You barely noticed I was there. You were too busy making eyes at your ex-lover and your cripple friend."

"You're nuts, you know that? You've really lost it."

"You don't want me," he said then, not hearing me, not hearing anything but the distorted music of his head. "You don't know how to love," he spat.

"I don't know how to love! You STOLE me from Bev, you came along and trounced through what we had, pissed on it as hard as you could, just to *amuse* yourself. You're like, 'Hey, there's a cute girl with a little confusion on the side, let's see how much we can RIP OFF HER HEAD AND FUCK HER NECK HOLE.' This is just a game for you. A tiny pastime to make the weeks slip by. Bev was right. You're the fucking devil. You feed off decay and dissolution, don't you? Don't you? Answer me, you asshole."

"Oh, come off it, you weren't happy with him. You were going nowhere. I did a lot for you. Come here." He yanked on my arm, trying to pull me to him.

"Get the fuck away from me," I hissed. He kept coming, though. So I slapped him. The sound of it rang out in midrange notes that splattered through the room. Rage spat out of his eyes and then he turned, picked up the phone, and started dialing furiously, banging the number pads as if they were my face.

"Who the fuck are you calling? What are you doing?"

"I'm calling the cops. I want you REMOVED. You HIT me."

"Grow the fuck up," I said. And that was it. One minute I was lying on Satan's red couch, mourning my father's death. The next minute, Satan went nuts, I slapped him, and it was over. Time to go home. I walked out, out of his bourgeois little townhouse. Out. Down Eleventh Street. Into a cab.

I went home, got into bed, and stayed there for a week. I did not answer the phone, write fuck books, or even let my maid in to clean my hovel. My neighbor Eye Girl, now in possession of a new boyfriend, whom I was tentatively thinking of as The Potato—Eye Girl and The Potato were fighting. They were screaming and throwing couches. At least they were communicating. During the very few seconds I allowed myself to think of Satan at all, it was the failure to communicate that stung me most. One minute we were walking the serrated edges of intimacy, the next minute I was walking away from his house never to return. Where was the segue?

On the eighth night after the Satan Debacle, Oliver appeared at my door and would not leave. He forced me to come out for an Idiots Anonymous dinner.

Hearing the other Idiots blather out their problems soothed me. Merle confessed to OD'ing on cookies. Beverly the Alcoholic told us she was convinced she had a brain tumor. She was, she said, going to move in with her great-aunt in the Ozarks and go on a fast. She was going to starve the brain tumor away, she said. Merle talked her down: "Beverly, I doubt you have a brain tumor, but if you think you do, go to the doctor. Fasting in the Ozarks is probably not the cure."

"Merle," Beverly said, exasperated, "you don't get it. I don't do doctors. Doctors are thinly veiled psychos and perverts. I'm going to take herbs and fast."

"Beverly, I just don't think you have a brain tumor. I mean, the first six months after I stopped shooting dope, I thought I had AIDS, cancer, and yes, a brain tumor."

Beverly looked down her nose at him.

"You just don't *get it*," she said impatiently.

Then, as Merle continued to try to dissuade Beverly from fasting in the Ozarks, I noticed the busboy. Everything lifted in that instant. After a slumber, Lust had come back. And its return banished Pain.

The busboy was shoveling plates off a nearby table. He did this beautifully.

"You slut," Oliver whispered, catching me mid-ogle. "Stop looking at him, you're heartbroken and grieving."

"Shhhhh," I said, putting my finger to his lips. The busboy turned around just then, looked at me, and smiled a sort of bewildered, deer-in-headlights smile.

"Rebound on me, Zoe," Oliver said in my ear as the busboy scurried to the kitchen and Elizabeth tried to convey to us the full importance of her obsession with yet another toothless guy.

"Oh, Ollie, I'd like to but I can't," I told him.

"You can, Zoe, you can," he said. We were speaking very quietly. In the background Elizabeth, ever eloquent, was citing the current toothless specimen's utter devotion to her as the most powerful stimulant her libido had ever encountered.

"I can't, Ollie," I said softly, "not with you. There's no suspension of disbelief. I know you too well. You know me. That makes it awkward. I can't project onto you. It won't work. Not now. In ten years. We'll be tired of this. We'll be tired of being Idiots. We'll fuck each other senseless and love each other, too. But not now."

Oliver sighed. Elizabeth was still expounding. The busboy was clearing another table.

By the end of our dinner, all the Idiots had spilled their guts. Except me. I couldn't voice it yet. We paid the check. We shook hands and kissed cheeks. We went our separate ways.

I went home and got back into bed. Then I thought of the busboy. I put my clothes back on. I walked back to the restaurant. The busboy was clearing a table. I handed him a note on which I'd scribbled my phone number. He looked bewildered. I went home again. Twenty minutes later, the phone rang.

"You didn't tell me your name," he said when I answered the phone.

"No. I didn't. What time do you get off work?"

"Now."

"Ah. Could I buy you a cup of tea?"

"Tea?"

"Tea."

"Sure."

The busboy looked good sipping tea. He looked good when we wordlessly walked back to my hovel. He walked like he was fucking. He was sturdy. Not fat, not thin, sturdy. He had a wide and slightly puffy mouth. As we walked down Avenue A, a gaggle of passing girls in tiny T-shirts ogled him. As we turned left onto Sixth Street, a guitar-toting babe with pink hair said hello to him. Had we walked a few more blocks, someone would have fucked him right there on the street.

Lonette and her kids were scrambling out of the building when we walked in. "Girl, you seen that motherfucking super around?" Lonette queried of me.

"Uh, no, I haven't," I said. It was nearly one in the morning. The super, presumably, was asleep.

"Motherfucker supposed to come look at my fucking ceiling," Lonette said.

"Well, I haven't seen him," I reiterated. Lonette grumbled, swatted at one of her kids' heads, then suddenly noticed the busboy. She looked him up and down. "Damn, where you find THAT?" she said.

The busboy favored her with a slow smile. I pushed through the front door, and as Lonette panted, the busboy followed me into the hall and up the stairs.

As I turned the key in my apartment door, the busboy pressed against my ass and bit into the back of my neck. I stood perfectly still. His hand came around to the front of my pants and began to unbutton them. I wondered if he had an exceptionally long dick. I could feel it pressing between my ass cheeks. He pulled my pants down. At any moment, Mikey the Heavy Metal Guitarist or Daisy the Fading Stripper or Eye Girl or anyone at all could have found us there. Me with my ass bare. The busboy with a tent in his pants. As it was, they did not. We could have fucked on the filthy hallway carpet and no one would have seen us. But, thanks to AIDS, we did not fuck on the filthy carpet. We went inside the apartment to get a condom. We took our shoes off and put the condom on the busboy's dick, which was not exceptionally long but possessed a pleasing width and a beautiful olive skin tone. Then we fucked. On the couch. Me on top. Riding him hard. Then soft. I came. He pulled me around to his side. Then he got on top. Put my legs on his shoulders. Formed an incredibly beautiful O with his mouth. Then came.

Then we talked. I said, "Are you hungry?" He said, "Yeah."

I produced a bowl of fruit salad from the fridge. He made a face and said, "I want candy."

For the next week, he came over each night after work. He liked to watch The Cartoon Network. He was especially fond of Scooby Doo. I'd feed him peanut butter cups in bed. Eventually, we told each other our names. His was Mark. But he was not Mark for long. For, the second time we slept together, when I asked if he'd read Denis Johnson, he flapped his beautiful eyes at me and said, "How would you feel if I told you I never read?" Then he became The Reader. He was a sweet Reader. Not big on conversation or personal disclosure. And a fascinating experiment. I wanted to see how far I could go with it. How long could we fuck without emotional tethers?

Two weeks went by. Finally, one day, my father's ashes came in the mail. Lucy the Mailwoman buzzed me. "Please come down, you have a package."

When I went down I saw a small cardboard box on the floor. Lucy had put my father's ashes on the filthy tenement hallway's floor. I didn't say anything, though. I didn't say, "Hey, that's my dad." I signed for my father's remains and went back up to the apartment. I did not open the box up. I put it on the windowsill. I didn't know what else to do with it. I didn't know what Charlie wanted me to do. I decided to wait till it came to me.

That night, when The Reader came over, I unraveled. Not a lot. I just said, "That's my dad," pointing to the box of ashes on the windowsill. The Reader held me then. He smoothed my hair and kissed the back of my head. In doing so, he let in Tenderness and our Experiment in Emotionless Fucking had come to an end. There was a feeling between us.

18

Fuck Me

And now here we are. Back in the closet. With the chain in my lap. I am thinking of Bev now. Bev with his close-cropped pale hair. Bev from whom Satan snatched me. Why did I let him? Because, you guessed it, I'm an emotional idiot. Because Repulsion and Attraction are strange bedfellows, married through the ages and, by turns, in love and in hate with each other but weathering all, staying together, the both of them now crinkly eyed ancients, entwined, intermingled, indelibly and forever. Because it is their marriage that defines emotional idiocy. Because it is from them that I have been born and through them have been formed so that I come to you now, singing off-key, a naked idiot, for all the world to see. See me, touch me, feed me, fuck me. And take out the garbage while you're at it.

That is why.

The last time I talked to Bev was a few weeks ago. I had E-mailed him a note saying "How are you?" Which, on the surface, may seem harmless, but the subtext of this innocent "How are you?" was "I hope you are lost without me, I hope you turn to Prozac, flail aimlessly through a boiling sea of imbeciles, and end up a headless torso in the pine box of love."

But Bev wouldn't play my little game. He E-mailed me back saying only this: "Please, Zoe, PLEASE."

I didn't know exactly how to interpret this. Did this "Please, Zoe,

PLEASE" imply that I was still pulling on his heartstrings? Or did it mean "Leave me alone, go fall off a building and die"?

I wasn't sure.

Then, a few days after all this, illumination came. I was walking down Houston Street with Oliver. Oliver and I were having a pleasant talk about the vagaries of love. We were trying to get to the bottom of why I was still pining for Bev. Then, as we walked, arms entwined, a gaggle of girls started walking ahead of us. They were attractive in that all-American way that makes me itch. They weren't *my* type, that's for sure. They were walking and giggling and they were all sporting those itty-bitty backpacks that are so fashionable these days. Suddenly a girl can't have a purse or a regular-sized backpack, she has to have an itty-bitty packpack. They are not functional. They are not attractive. They represent something formidably malevolent.

Oliver then pointed to the girl with the ittiest-bittiest backpack and said, "See those itty-bitty backpacks? They're navigational devices for young girls. Inside the backpack is a microchip that programs their behavior and also helps them to locate each other. That's why those backpacks are so popular now."

Just then one of the girls made a funny twitching gesture with her arm. "Aha, look at that," Oliver said, "her backpack made her twitch like that. Soon people will be *breeding* inside itty-bitty backpacks. They'll just start lopping off their genitals, sticking 'em inside the itty-bitty backpacks with the genitals of someone they find attractive, and they will breed more people just like them."

"Yeah," I said then, "they can't function without backpacks, and I bet they all think they're fat even though they're not. They wear itty-bitty backpacks and gulp huge vats of Slim-Fast and fantasize about being stranded in Ethiopia." Oliver laughed at that and then, because these girls were being annoyingly loud but also because Oliver, like me, has a sadistic streak, as we passed the gaggle of girls, Oliver said loudly, "God, what a FAT bunch of girls."

The girls totally flipped then. They stopped in their tracks and all started grabbing their thighs, as if they had suddenly been STRUCK FAT.

But those girls unwittingly got even with me because I right then happened to notice that on the back of the girl with the ittiest-bittiest backpack's pack was a sticker for Bev's band, Lotus Crew. The Itty-Bitty Backpack Chick was advertising Bev's band on her postage-stamp-sized backpack. The fact of this encapsulated *all* my fears. That Bev was not pining for me. That I could *never* get him back if I tried because he was in fact busy having sex with an Itty-Bitty Backpack Chick and had better things to do than E-mail me, and his writing me a note that said "Please, Zoe, PLEASE" in fact meant "Please go away, I'm too busy with my Itty-Bitty Backpack Chicks, buzz off."

"Oliver," I wailed, turning to my friend, "Oliver, Bev is fucking an Itty-Bitty Backpack Chick, isn't he?"

"Oh, Zoe, you're being dramatic. No one could go from fucking you to fucking someone with an itty-bitty backpack. It just isn't done." This is why I love Oliver.

A few days passed after this. Out of the blue, Bev suddenly decided to call me on the phone for the first time in months. "Hi, Zoe, it's Bev," he said. After a few minutes of pleasantries, I went for the heart of the matter.

"Bev?"

"Yeah?"

"You're not by any chance sleeping with a girl with an itty-bitty backpack, are you?"

"Wow," Bev said. "Good call."

I hung up pretty quickly after that. I sat at my desk, staring at a half-finished fuck book manuscript and realizing that the fact of Bev doing it with Itty-Bitty Backpack Chicks really ought to break the spell. That I really ought to be able to let go now. Logically speaking.

But logic has nothing to do with any of this. Logic would not have me sitting in my ex-boyfriend's closet, dreaming of tying him up and demeaning him and, in the next breath, thinking of appearing at my ex-boyfriend Bev's doorstep to grovel, to say "I was wrong, lash me and take me back."

Of course, Bev probably has an Itty-Bitty Backpack Chick in his bed as we speak. And, well, I'm glad. I loved him. I still love him. I want him to be happy. I want him to breed an entire tribe of itty-bitty backpack people if that's what will make him happy. I loved Edgar and Oliver and Nicholas the Horse Thief and John the Garbageman and Max, and obviously I loved Satan. I loved everybody. And now I will push on, scrubbing the metaphoric toilets of love.

And I don't know what the fuck I am doing here. I don't want to chain Satan to his bed. I should probably try eating healthier and sleeping more. I'm fucking psycho.

That's it. I'm outta here. What was I thinking? What if he came home while I was still here? What the fuck would I do then?

I put the chain back in the bag. I emerge from the closet. I walk down the stairs and out onto the landing. I dutifully lock Satan's door behind me. A cab is pulling up. Of course. It's Satan. He hasn't seen me yet. He is paying the cabdriver. He is getting a receipt. If ever the IRS audits Satan, they will find his devilish whereabouts well documented.

"What are you doing here?" Satan says, seeing me.

"Uh, I came to uh . . . get some stuff. My shirt. I left my blue shirt in your house."

"Oh. Well, you might have called."

"Yeah, well, yeah. I thought about it but I needed my shirt."

"Where's my chair?"

"What?"

"My *chair*, the gray office chair, that was a *loan*. I want my chair back."

"No, I need it."

"It's *my* chair," Satan says, his little Lucifer eyes brightening at the prospect of a fight.

"I'm going to burn your chair," I say. Satan's face twitches then. Nothing gets to him as much as a threat to his property. Even if just to a measly gray office chair. I can see he's about to go nuts. He's about to lose it because I said I'd burn his chair.

What was I thinking? This is the guy I was going to chain up and watch squirm? I don't want to watch him squirm. I don't even want to burn his chair. I don't care about his chair.

"I'll send your chair back."

"I want you to bring it back."

"No, I'll UPS it," I say. Satan is perplexed at this.

"You can just *bring* it, no need to *send* it."

"I want to send it. I'm going to send it. Good-bye."

With that I turn and walk down Eleventh Street. I am still carrying the black plastic bag with my bike chain in it. I'm gonna go call The Reader. I will make him lie down and be quiet and I will read to him. Then I will fuck him and feed him cake. Or maybe not. Maybe I'll just go home alone and mind my own business. I'll stop trying to pretend that The Reader makes me happy. He doesn't. The experiment is over. Fucking without emotion only lasts a short while. And the emotions that now travel between The Reader and I, well, they're the sub-dwarfs of emotions. I like him. He is a walking fuck machine and this is pleasing. He's cute but you can have him. I am tired. I am going to sleep now. Without The Reader. He's practically illiterate. He won't even read this book.

Good-bye.